The Woman
at the Window

in memoriam
Richard Dynevor

The Woman at the Window

Emyr Humphreys

seren

Seren is the book imprint of
Poetry Wales Press Ltd
57 Nolton Street, Bridgend, Wales, CF31 3AE
www.seren-books.com

ISBN: 978-1-85411-489-1

This book is a work of fiction. The characters and incidents portrayed
are the work of the author's imagination. Any other resemblance to
actual persons, living or dead, is entirely coincidental.

Inner design and typesetting by logodædaly
Printed by Bell and Bain, Glasgow

The publisher works with the financial assistance of
The Welsh Books Council.

Contents

The Grudge

i

WITH Lord Parry of Penhesgyn there was no means of telling whether he was pleased to see you or pleased for you to see him. In his early seventies he was well preserved. The same broad thick-lipped smile could be discerned in old school photographs when he was an outstanding sixth-former and the smile had stood him in good stead throughout a long political career. In retirement there was little point in abandoning the attitude of a lifetime. He still enjoyed a fine head of white hair and an imposing if portly proconsular presence. He listened with a slight tilt of the head as though considering a petition that he would prefer to grant rather than reject if the government's finances would allow it.

He still liked to demonstrate democratic goodwill and throw back his distinguished head to indulge in rich baritone chuckles. He had held high office and even higher had been in reach but, as he was ready to confess, he lacked that streak of ruthlessness that makes it possible to plunge a knife in a colleague's back. In a sense he was a victim of his own irrepressible good nature. 'Alas' he would say. 'All political careers end in failure, so who am I to complain?'

His cousin, the crowned and chaired poet Gwilym Hesgyn, was altogether different. He looked like a man who had been whittled down by a lifetime of disappointments, and this in spite of his eisteddfodic triumphs. He sat in his study in his orchard bungalow staring at the magnificent view of the mountains, and longing for a fresh surge of inspiration that would prove once and for all and beyond question the unique qualities of his gift. The world had never sufficiently appreciated his vision or the lifetime of struggle and sacrifice he had devoted to preserving his heritage and his beloved commote of Hesgyn from alien invasion. His territory as much as his talent had been overrun by hostile forces: landmarks of the spirit had been bulldozed and replaced with unsightly evanescent structures. Farmsteads and fields with poetic, ancient names had been replaced by bungaloid developments occupied by newcomers with raucous voices and unruly children.

When he learned that his cousin, 'the noble lord' as he called him with monotonous sarcasm, had decided to retire to Plas Penhesgyn, it seemed to him a fresh insult to add to a lifetime of injury. The man dared to set himself up as a latterday lord of the manor and let it be known that his childhood haunts meant more to him than they could possibly mean to anyone else. It was to his long-suffering daughter Rhian Mai that Gwilym Hesgyn snarled:

'Return of the Native! Return of the Traitor more like.

The nerve of the man. The sheer brassnecked nerve!'

Rhian Mai trembled and held her breath. Nothing much had gone well for her since she made the dreadful mistake of marrying a charming but feckless Dane in the early eighties. Claus Fleming was unable to distinguish between fact and fiction, or as her father put it, 'he was a born liar'. For example, was he in fact a Dane or a German? He was born in Flensburg, but he told them that he wrote in German. He came to Hesgyn Bay to snorkle and remained, he said, to complete his best-selling thriller in the caravan he rented in their orchard. On the very site where the bungalow now stood with its wonderful view of the mountains. His book would be translated into fluent English and as many as twenty-three languages and without question make his fortune. It was Claus this and Claus that throughout that remarkable summer. The sky above him was always blue and the sun was his halo. Claus said his true love was poetry and he seemed to listen enthralled to Gwilym Hesgyn's exposition of the mysteries of cynghanedd and the twenty-four metres.

Father and daughter were taken in, although the father never admitted it. In the end the unpublished author went off to Thailand leaving a trail of debt and misery behind him. As Mrs Fleming she played the organ in Moriah chapel on alternate Sundays. She attended the evening Bible class conducted on Tuesday evenings by Catrin Dodd, the doctor's wife. This offered more than an escape from her father's rumbling discontent. She felt the need to explore a book that might lead her to the true nature of love and forgiveness: to forgive herself as much as her errant husband. It would help her to unravel the tightening knots of years of resentment.

For Rhian Mai the prospect of the return of a distinguished relative offered some relief on a social level. Ever since the collapse of her marriage she had moved around the district virtually on tiptoe for fear of disturbing some further consequence of Claus Fleming's irresponsible behaviour. To have an important uncle in residence might enable her to walk down the street with her head held a little higher. There remained such a thing as being well-connected.

'They say he's very nice. Tada!'

'Nice! Being nice is nothing. Any fool can be nice. Rogues and politicians make a speciality of being nice!'

Her patient and prayerful longing for peace and reconciliation in the wider family seemed answered when a printed invitation to a housewarming at Plas Penhesgyn arrived, with a handwritten note from his lordship, signed Clem, anticipating a friendly chat about the good old days and all the spirited adventures of their youth. It seemed that life could take a turn for the better, until her father's stubborn growl crushed her hopes.

'I don't want to smell the man let alone talk to him!'

Her father sank further into his rocking chair to nurse his resentment. From under overgrown eyebrows he glared at his daughter.

'You've got no idea,' he said. 'Not the slightest idea what I've had to put up with. All down the years. My mother thought the sun rose in his arse. The great hero of the family.

She dressed me in his reach-me-downs as if I were being handed down royal robes. Crippled my feet in his old football boots. Ruined any chance of my reaching the first eleven. He was captain of the school and nothing I did was ever good enough. Even when I won the chair he'd been elected to the English Parliament and my mother was convinced he'd be the next Prime Minister. All he ever had was a good memory. Photographic. I heard him say so himself. He could master a brief in record time and then chuck it away to make way for the next one. Just as he chucked principles away. Not to mention people!'

His discontents rumbled on. The peaceful routine in the orchard bungalow was often disrupted by the chaired bard's restless urge to devise means and methods, chiefly surreptitious, of exposing the shortcomings of his cousin: or the shabby subterfuges of that long political career. He fulminated, and at most mealtimes she had to listen.

'Justice must be rocklike! That's what I believe. The fulcrum of a civilised society. People should understand that.'

He cherished the phrases. He took time to hammer them out and in some sense saw them as part of his bardic mission.

'Rocklike,' he said. 'Otherwise it will melt. Evaporate. Blow away and be forgotten. Lost in the sand.'

For her own part Rhian Mai wondered if that indeed was the case. Not that she dared openly to disagree. Her father was too easily upset and driven into one of his rages of frustration. She racked her brains for some way of bringing up the case for reconciliation as a general principle. The sad

13

truth was since the failure of her marriage and all the troubles that went with it, her father was only too quick to demonstrate contempt for her lack of intellect and even common sense. She spent more time in chapel practising on the organ. She cherished the secret hope of discussing the nature of forgiveness on a one-to-one basis with the doctor's wife. More than her own shyness restrained her. There was no knowing what sleeping dogs of family disgrace would be disturbed if she started blurting everything out.

Catrin Dodd was a formidable woman who in Rhian Mai's eyes oozed success from every pore. She had given up her career in the University Department of Religious Studies in order to bring up three burly sons, and the fame of her achievement spread wide in Presbyterian circles. While she viewed the doctor's wife with admiration and awe, she found the doctor himself intimidating. Since he was a keen amateur practitioner of the strict metres he was a frequent visitor at the orchard bungalow calling, as he put it, to consult the oracle. As a past master of his art he paid Gwilym Hesgyn exaggerated respect. He had a loud voice, a jovial manner and a bulky presence. She was obliged to nod more than once when he repeated that her father in France would be addressed as 'Cher Maître'. She could never quite tell when the doctor was joking or being serious. Her father appeared to have no difficulty at all in making the distinction; beyond the study door she could hear his contented snigger punctuate the doctor's loud laughter. It was possible too much isolation had made her socially tone deaf.

The Grudge

In the Bible class Rhian Mai concentrated on being unobtrusive. There were teachers present as well as a philosophical market gardener. She judged herself the least educated among the group and certainly the person most in need of some form of spiritual sustenance. The others seemed able to chat lightheartedly among themselves. Their lives were so much brighter, more fulfilled than her own, and this was reflected in the ease and confidence of their discourse. Should David have taken steps more speedily to be reconciled with his son Absalom, and was Hushai just as guilty as Ahitophel of deception and double-dealing? And did it all fit in with the workings of Providence, or just a pattern of a national myth? All Rhian could think of was David's grief, and the tears welled up in her large and mournful eyes.

Her distress did not escape Catrin Dodd's notice. She was tempted to take her aside after the class and ask her if anything was troubling her. It was part of her remit to take a pastoral interest in her students. Mrs Fleming had allowed herself to murmur aloud that if families couldn't get on how could the family of nations be expected to live in peace with each other? This was sufficient to determine Catrin Dodd on a course of action. The following morning, at breakfast, the doctor's wife urged her husband to tackle Gwilym Hesgyn at the first opportunity.

'He's a bad-tempered old misery guts at the best of times,' she said. 'He's making his daughter's life miserable. He listens to you. Use your authority. Tell the old man to think of his daughter. Tell him selfishness is bad for his health. He's so monumentally thoughtless and he calls himself a poet. Tell him to let bygones be bygones – or whatever.'

'Is that an edict?'

His wife was adding to his workload but he approached the task in his usual cheerful manner. He had a couple of new leaflets on blood pressure and the treatment of the prostate gland; also an englyn sequence of his own that he would like Gwilym Hesgyn to take a critical look at. Armed with these he paid the poet a visit. The doctor found the chaired bard in his study studying the list of subjects for the next National Eisteddfod but one, which had arrived with the morning post.

'Well now then Gwilym Hesgyn! How about it? Doesn't the ever-changing light on the mountains inspire you? What a subject! I will lift up mine eyes unto the hills. You've only got to sit here and set the pulse of composition racing!'

He advanced to the window and made large gestures suggesting an inexhaustible source of inspiration.

'It's been done before,' Gwilym Hesgyn said. 'Too often if you ask me. Talking of pulse I think my pressure is going up. Do you think the tablets are strong enough?'

The doctor reassured him that his tablets were of adequate strength. He added the poet would be well advised to take more exercise now that the weather had improved. And perhaps he should drink more soda-water and cranberry juice. When his mind was at rest concerning his blood pressure Gwilym Hesgyn launched himself into an unsparing critique of the doctor's metrical sequence. Quite apart from technical deficiencies, he felt the subject matter was too frivolous. The doctor should dig deeper to find deeper thoughts. The doctor shook his head. He accepted all technical criticism cheerfully, but digging deeper didn't appeal.

'I'll tell you the advice old Prof Oliver gave me when I told him I was going into general practice. "Remember to keep your patients at a decent arm's length," he said. "It's their bodies you are paid to cure, not their souls." Well I feel the same about thoughts, Gwilym Hesgyn. If they lie too deep for tears, let them lie there.'

He gave a roar of laughter that puzzled the poet and then made a sudden change of subject.

'I hear your noble cousin is settling down very nicely. Don't you think it's time you paid him a visit?'

Gwilym Hesgyn bared his teeth as though the doctor had just made a joke.

'Take Mrs Fleming with you. It would do her good. She's been looking rather anaemic lately, don't you think?'

'He had a nerve to come back here. After all the things he's done. People forget things. That's one thing about poets, Doctor Gronw. They don't forget. Their business is to remember. Never forget the present rests on the foundation of the past.'

The doctor frowned as he considered the proposition.

'You never met Eiry'r Mynydd? No of course not. You're too young.'

The doctor showed signs of vague recognition.

'You wrote a poem sequence about her.'

'Of course I did. Bright and beautiful she was. A glorious symbol. Her home was in a valley threatened with inundation. We tried to save it. We struggled. We protested. We fought. And who was in the vanguard making the Cause his very own? My cousin Clement Parry. Hero of the hour. And Eiry fell in love with him unfortunately. But when the real testing time came and a prison sentence in the offing, the great Clement became unavailable. Gone off to America on a Fulbright.'

'Well there you are,' the doctor said. 'The story with so many politicians.'

Gwilym Hesgyn was unappeased.

'It's worse than that. When he comes back he dumps her. Breaks her heart. And why, you ask? In order to marry the daughter of a Labour Lord and inherit a safe seat. That's the kind of fellow he is. A sly, duplicitous bastard.'

'But he's your cousin, Gwilym Hesgyn! Don't forget that!'

'I don't intend to forget anything. People may forget, but I don't. And I'll tell you more. I've got chapter and verse written down. Look here.'

Trembling with energy and indignation, from a bureau he produced a black ledger and waved it in the air.

'Did you know the last time that man was in office he issued a contract to Intruder Services and within six months of leaving the government he was on their board!'

'That's politicians,' the doctor said. 'Most of them do it.'

'And the way they treat him! Honorary this and that. The University. The Eisteddfod. Instead of being punished he gets institutionalised. I'm going to give him his just desserts. An honest account of our hero's life and work. In the strict metres. A technical tour de force and at the same time the branding iron of fact!'

He was pleased with himself and waited for the doctor to share his pleasure with a robust laugh. Instead the doctor frowned and shook his head as he did when facing an unpromising diagnosis.

'Where would you get a thing like that published? Libel and all that?'

Gwilym Hesgyn tapped his nose and put his fingers to his lips.

ii

The public lecture which Lord Parry kindly agreed to deliver was very well received: particularly so among the growing numbers of retired English that Gwilym Hesgyn described as 'Settlers'. The title of the lecture also enraged him. *The Second Chamber: an intimate view*. 'Their House of Lords, isn't it?' he fumed. 'Public Lecture indeed! Anything that gives them an excuse to cluster. In no time at all they'll form a caucus and take the place over, County Council included!' Rhian Mai would have loved to attend the lecture but she dared not risk her father's displeasure. The doctor and his wife were present and to their surprise enjoyed the occasion.

Lord Parry was still impressive to look at and easy to listen to. He played an audience like an instrument, making a virtuoso's use of pauses and hesitations as well as his rich baritone. In no time he extracted laughter with nicely judged touches of self-deprecation; and then nostalgia and fond memories with a hint of sadness in order to end on a note of universal goodwill. The applause verged on the rapturous and comparisons were made with notable orators of the past and a mysterious quality called Dawn Môn.

At the modest reception afterwards Lord Parry circulated graciously among the invited. An important-looking matron introduced him to the doctor and his wife! 'Dr Gronw Dodd? Author of *Medical Matters among the Morisiaid*? Could they be one and the same?' It seemed they shared a lifelong interest in the Morris letters. And even when Lord Parry turned his attention to Catrin and learned about her academic past and her knowledge of Hebrew, he was able to recall an official visit to the Holy Land, and how, for ever after, he enjoyed nothing more than browsing in the Old Testament and comparing the various translations. There was so much of mutual interest to talk about, the doctor and his wife were pressed to dine with him at the earliest opportunity. 'Take pity on a lonely old man,' he said with a cheerful smile. In spite of reservations, Doctor Gronw and his wife Catrin were equally charmed. It was not every day of the week you came across an ex-member of the government showing such a civilised breadth of interests, so much interest in Old Testament texts and the Morris letters.

They agreed that Lord Parry of Penhesgyn knew how to win friends and influence people.

The dinner party they attended at Plas Penhesgyn was a pleasant occasion. Eight persons of consequence sat at the round table and Catrin was flattered to find herself seated next to her host. The meal was prepared by Kazimeira and her daughter Maria. 'Polish exiles, guest workers if you like,' Lord Parry explained to Catrin. 'Inclined to be emotional but excellent cooks... as you can judge by their size.' He made further asides in a language the two women had no claim to understanding. 'They are prone to bouts of hiraeth and to sudden quarrels. Then they are quickly reconciled. Usually in floods of tears. Never a dull moment!' Catrin would have liked to pick up on the theme of reconciliation, but the wife of the Principal of the Further Education College had raised her voice to ask a cheerful question. 'Why were the things going on backstage always more interesting than the political shadow-boxing taking place in front of the footlights?' Soon the company was enjoying a rich sequence of anecdotes and revelations. As the wine flowed they were warmed by a sense of privilege and well-being. The Principal's wife was emboldened to ask his lordship what in his opinion made a good politician? His reply was only tangential, but he had used it before and found it effective.

'Broadly speaking you can divide politicians into two classes. Those who expect to serve their country and those who expect their country to serve them. I leave you to decide which camp I belong to!'

Doctor Gronw established such cordial terms with Lord Clement Parry that in the course of time it became just as easy for him to drop in at Plas Penhesgyn as at Gwilym Hesgyn's orchard bungalow. There were minor indispositions to attend to, particularly with the Polish women, and Lord Parry was so grateful for the doctor's help that he urged him to call him 'Clem'.

After the first jovial flush of comradeship and the occasional convivial session, Gronw confessed to his wife that this new-found friendship made him uneasy. He felt that he was being false at both ends and getting nowhere near Catrin's cherished goal of reconciliation in Rhian Mai's extended family.

'I don't really care so much about the two old men,' she said. 'It's Mrs Fleming I worry about. The poor thing is suffering. It's all so unnecessary.'

In the depth of a leather armchair in Lord Parry's well-appointed study, Doctor Gronw resolved to speak up. He balanced a cup of coffee in his large hands, smiled at Polish Maria and glanced briefly at the weather vane above the gable end of the coach house. Not for the first time he compared this limited view with the inspirational panorama to be seen through the window of Gwilym Hesgyn's far more modest and crowded study in the orchard bungalow.

'You know Clem, you could drop in on your cousin Gwilym. Tell him how much you admire his poetry. That sort of thing. It would do the old boy no end of good.'

Lord Parry parried the petition with ease. 'Why not? I might indeed do that.'

He had things of greater urgency on his mind that he was eager to discuss with the doctor. A local sense of renewal had to be set in motion. Things had been allowed to slide and there was a need for a positive approach. The village green, for example, where he and his companions of yore had played from dawn until dusk, had been invaded by gorse bushes. They bloomed right up to the War Memorial that itself stood in need of refurbishing. It was in the shape of a Celtic Cross and the names of the Fallen were literally falling off the marble plinth or fading away. Then again the old church school that served as a Pensioners' club badly needed doing up. Why not encourage the natives and the settlers to engage in friendly rivalry in a programme of renewal. He put forward a range of stimulating ideas. The doctor could not but agree.

It was on his next visit, urged on by his wife, that the doctor grew more persistent. If there was to be a renewal, he argued, why not start with a reconciliation?

'You can move from a position of strength, Clem. The mark of the magnanimous is to show mercy. That sort of thing. You know what I mean.'

Lord Parry took a deep breath, shook his head more in sorrow than in anger, and moved forward in his chair as though he did not wish to be overheard.

'My cousin Gwil was born timid, you see. That meant he got bullied. In school I always had to defend him. More or less take him under my wing.'

'Well there you are then!' Doctor Gronw was jubilant as if a magic solution had presented itself.

'Let me tell you something, Gronw, and let it go no further.' Lord Parry's voice grew deep and solemn.

'There was a time when Gwilym was in real trouble. And the truth is he has never forgiven me for getting him out of it. He got a headship in Powys. Years ago. Could be on the strength of his eisteddfodic triumphs. Anyway he got on the wrong side of the dinner ladies. As you may have noticed he never found it difficult to get on the wrong side of anybody. He was, you may say, hell-bent on getting a second eisteddfod chair. I suppose people had been telling him he was a genius. He wished to be the biggest fish in his little literary pool. His head was more in the clouds than usual: the dinner money went missing, evaporated in one way or another, and the dinner ladies laid all the blame on him. He was suspended. There was an enquiry and his mother, poor woman, implored me to get him out of trouble. Which I did. I had a devil of a job keeping the whole affair out of court. And he's never ceased to resent being grateful all those years. That's the true source of the grudge, and that's my cousin for you. Eaten up with envy and resentment. So what can I do about it?'

Gronw Dodd was lost for an answer. He stared into his coffee as though the brown liquid had become an inexplicable mystery.

iii

The doctor decided not to let the ancient quarrels of two old men weigh on his stomach. They were so hardened in their attitudes it would need steel chisels to prise them out of them. This was not an operation he had been trained for. For the time being he would give both of them a wide berth. He had more than enough to do with patients in physical predicaments he could do something about. Even in the case of Mrs Fleming he could alleviate her menopausal discomforts. To make up for being deprived of exercises in the strict metres he could immerse himself in pharmaceutical literature, and write out more sophisticated prescriptions. A doctor in general practice needed to cultivate a degree of detachment, otherwise he could get bogged down in emotional quagmires of incalculable depth. He should allow the human comedy to become an amusing diversion from the daily irritations of the National Health Service and the machinations of political parties bent on persuading a gullible public that they had an inalienable right to live for ever.

At breakfast, as he was bracing himself to face the rigours of another heavy day, his wife Catrin once again brought up the vexed subject.

'I'm very worried about Rhian Mai,' she said. 'She takes everything so much to heart.'

'Those two old donkeys...'

Doctor Gronw chewed faster on his toast.

'Someone ought to knock their heads together.'

'It's worse than that. She's had a letter from her ex-husband. She showed it to me after class. Poor thing must have been desperate to do that. Didn't know who to turn to. Terrified her father might see it.'

'What did it say? The letter?'

'Basically he's demanding money.'

'Of course. What else. Don't they all. That sort.'

'He says he has a son from his marriage in Thailand and wants to educate him. He wants six thousand right away to pay the boy's fees. He says he part owns the orchard bungalow. Helped to build it he claims. She says it isn't true. I said why don't you show the letter to your uncle? He's a distinguished lawyer. She's much too scared to do so. The poor thing is like a rabbit in a trap.'

Contemplating the depth of Rhian Mai's misery reduced them both to silence. The doctor could escape to his appointments in the surgery but for Catrin that misery invaded the comfortable house like a mist that refused to clear. She attempted some preparation for the Tuesday evening class but the dire warnings made by minor prophets seemed to apply even more to individuals than to nations, chosen or otherwise. Could it be that Rhian Mai was being made to pay for her innocence. Was youthful folly so culpable? And how youthful and how innocent? How are such shortcomings quantified. She concluded that Rhian Mai was the victim of the rampaging selfishness and egomania of untamed males. Satan's willing accomplices. Could the coefficient of woe in the human condition remain constant down the centuries? Rhian Mai's distress was here and now.

Catrin Dodd lost patience with speculation. Theory without practice was useless. She had to do something. To act. She would confront the monster in his lair, interfering or not. She set off in her little car, her heart thudding in her breast. The lane to the orchard bungalow was narrow and her heart beat even faster when she was confronted with an ambulance with its blue lights already flashing. In her anxiety to get out of the way she reversed her on-side rear wheel into the ditch. The ambulance driver waved an angry fist and it was quite clear he was swearing at her. Then one of the paramedics recognised the doctor's wife. She was relieved to get out of the car while they lifted the rear wheel out. She found Rhian Mai sitting in the ambulance and trembling from head to foot. Her father was the casualty. He lay on the stretcher bed with a drip in his arm and an oxygen mask on his face. She whispered down to Catrin standing in the lane: 'I thought he was going to kill me. I really did. He was raving and raging and smashing ornaments with his stick. And then he fell over and couldn't get up. Couldn't speak.'

Catrin drove behind the ambulance the twelve-mile journey to the general hospital. While they tried to keep up with the trolley down the long corridor from Emergency to Intensive Care, Rhian Mai clung to her arm and could not stop shivering. Catrin commandeered a red blanket, led her to the canteen and made her drink a cup of hot, sweet tea. Bit by bit she was able to put together a coherent account of what had happened.

'I wasn't out of the house an hour.... When I came back he was waving Claus' letter in my face and calling me all sorts of things I can't repeat. He said I had been in touch with him all these years and when I denied it he called me a liar and a two-faced whore. It was awful. The way he worked himself up. What made it all worse in a way was that building the bungalow in the orchard was Claus' idea in the first place. He was full of ideas...'

A blush on her cheeks betrayed a lingering admiration for her ex-husband that had to be corrected.

'He never paid for anything. Never. He had this way of handling my father. He drew a plan of the bungalow and marked out where it should stand to give the best view of the mountains. "A proper dwelling for a major poet," he said. My father loved listening to him. He pretended to take so much interest in poetry. Maybe he did, of course. There was no telling with Claus. He could get round anybody. My father always blamed me for his disappointment. And now this is my fault.'

'It is not. And it never was. And you mustn't ever think that.' Catrin concluded it was time to exert a little authority. Rhian Mai stared at her so gratefully, welcoming any reproof. This was a woman who had never taken charge of her own life, never exercised her duty to herself. There were things to do and Catrin Dodd would show her how they were done. Back at the orchard bungalow, once the broken ornaments were cleared up, she took possession of the offending letter.

'Lord Parry must see this,' she said. 'He's a lawyer. He will know exactly what to do.'

Rhian Mai sat in an armchair sipping more tea and

mumbling her thanks. She had no idea what she would have done without Mrs Dodd's help.

At the hospital, Gwilym Hesgyn's condition was stabilised sufficiently for him to be shunted into a side ward. He was conscious but unable to speak. His gaze followed the nurses with relentless suspicion. He did not appear to recognise anyone. Not even his own daughter. He stared at her as if she were a dangerous intruder. Squashing his bulk into a corner of the cramped side ward, Doctor Dodd studied the patient's reactions with great interest. Outside, when Rhian Mai in desperation sought explanations, he shook his head wisely and declared strokes were a mystery.

'He'll need a brain scan of course,' he said. 'But that won't explain everything. How could it? It's like consciousness really. Whoever defined that? All we can do is give it time and hope for the best.'

Sitting alone in her father's study and staring at the view that she believed belonged to him, Rhian Mai was visited by her own flash of inspiration. She would take a copy of her father's first book, *Hesgyn Harvest*, on her next visit. He would be sure to recognise his own verses. They were so memorable. Catrin Dodd was delighted at the idea. It was a sign that henceforward Rhian Mai would be capable of initiative. She arrived at the hospital clutching the book in one hand and Catrin Dodd's arm in the other. When the stiff door of the side ward opened they discovered Gwilym Hesgyn already had a visitor. Lord Parry of Penhesgyn had been provided with a chair and sat holding the patient's emaciated hand in both his own. A rigid diagonal smile was fixed on Gwilym Hesgyn's face. They could see Lord Parry's eyes were watering.

'He recognised me,' Lord Parry said. 'Straight away. No trouble at all.'

The Woman at the Window

THE woman in black stood at the drawing-room window of the Old Rectory, contemplating the landscape. What she saw, as far as she knew, could not think or feel but it endured the passage of the seasons more successfully than she did. Spring would arrive with renewed strength, disturbing the soil. She raised a hand to her neck and smoothed her cheek as if to disperse a pressure on her skin. In the middle-distance she could see the white sails of a windmill, recently refurbished to attract tourists, show above the undulating hedges and, further to the north, four turbines of the wind farm to which her late husband had taken such exception. 'Damn them,' he said. 'Ruining my skyline.' Now they were as much part of the view from the drawing-room window as the thin glimpse of the Irish Sea beyond them.

Even as she stared a stranger appeared, opening the road gate. He walked silently along the sweep of gravel drive towards the house. He wore a black coat and hat and walked with a seemly hesitation in his step, like a man about to attend a funeral. His solemn figure contrasted with the rows of daffodils in full bloom that glistened in the fitful sunlight. She could see her husband's cat, Bella, padding down the drive to greet the visitor. She had been lost in thought for so long she had forgotten to feed her. The stranger was pleased to kneel and stroke the luxurious fur of the appealing creature. Before she could issue any warning the man had been scratched and bitten for his pains.

When she opened the door she was confronted by a middle-aged visitor with a craggy face and a row of ingratiating small teeth. He was nursing a small wound on his left hand before raising his hat.

'That frightful cat,' she said. 'She can be so vicious when she's not fed. My fault I suppose. I forget to feed her.'

He bowed awkwardly and hung on to the hat he was not used to wearing.

'Mrs Picton?'

There could have been some doubt. She nodded.

'Of course,' he said. 'Of course. I know it's a fortnight late. But I heard nothing you see. I was out of touch in the middle of nowhere. In Sicily actually. But I felt I had to pay my respects. Please accept my deepest sympathy.'

She murmured her thanks but as he spoke it was clear she had no idea who her visitor might be. Perhaps because of his dark clothes and sparse grey hair he could have been an old-fashioned bank manager or a headmaster who had taken early retirement.

'Anwyl,' he said. 'Elwyn Anwyl. You could say I was Huw's oldest friend. One of them anyway. He was always very popular. I was his first partner anyway. It feels awful to have missed his funeral. So I had to come.'

The widow pointed to the wounds on his hand.

'Better put something on them,' she said. 'You never know where that blessed cat has been. She spends most of the time in the churchyard.'

Through the skeletal row of leafless trees he could glimpse the crumbling stone wall that separated the rectory garden from a churchyard on a lower elevation. An easy wall to climb over. The old parish church looked far smaller than the forbidding grey stone rectory. They were both isolated buildings at the centre of a rambling rural parish.

'Huw used to call me El Al. Does that ring a bell I wonder?'

It did not. A nickname seemed a poor proof of identity. He looked flustered as though he were rummaging through his mind for more convincing credentials. She was the widow, clearly on home ground. He was no more than a strange man calling at the front door.

'If you come in I could put some TCP on your hand.'

He breathed deeply with the relief of gratitude. The interior, as much as he could see of it, was dim and sparsely furnished. The kitchen on the other hand, when they reached it, was surprisingly new. It gleamed in the slanting light like an illustration from a brochure.

'What a marvellous kitchen.'

He spoke with polite enthusiasm.

'Well appointed and virtually unused,' she said, 'and still to be paid for. You've come a long way?'

'Well yes. I have. From Ravenna. So shocked when I read

the obit. The newspaper from home is a week old when I get it. And you could call me computer illiterate. And as I said I'd been in Sicily. Not just shock. Remorse. Regret. We'd been close you see, all those years ago. He was always so fit and so full of life. I had no idea he was ill.'

'Neither had I,' she said. 'A massive stroke. They could do nothing. One minute he was here. The next he was gone.'

'Here.'

Elwyn Anwyl repeated the word as though to make it echo in the space the friend of his younger days had vacated.

'For so long I'd been meaning to get in touch, I wanted him to know how much our friendship had meant to me, in spite of everything. And now it's too late.'

He became absorbed in regretful silence. She stood with her arms folded contemplating a complete stranger replete with a chapter of her husband's life of which she apparently knew nothing.

'I saw him first at the Debates Union. Reddish-yellow hair. He had a radiance about him. A figure of envy. A brilliant speaker with a wonderful self-effacing style that made you envy him even more. I admired him from a distance. We didn't actually connect up until a comic incident in the BBC Club in Langham Place. I don't know whether it's still there. A fine day outside and for some reason everyone inside slightly drunk. Huw was engaged in a furious argument with a beanpole of a man with a small head and a permanent sneer who maintained there was nothing worth knowing in Welsh literature otherwise the whole world would know about it. I joined in and we floored him to our own satisfaction. After that we were friends for life. Or at least we were until we fell out.'

She listened with detached interest, until she heard the cat meowing outside the door.

'I must feed that beastly cat. Otherwise who knows what she'll get up to.'

He was left in the glow of his own recollections. She was more concerned with the cat than a stranger's memories of her husband. Bereavement had left her in shock perhaps: an arrested state, certainly aware of the surface of existence but not able to react to her own awareness. She had been listening closely enough. The passage of years left such yawning gaps. No accumulation of the past could relieve the exigencies of the present; feeding the cat could loom as a major operation. That seemed true enough. She had fed the cat and now she could attend to him.

'Would you like a coffee? I'm afraid I've only got Nescafe.'

She gave him further information as she discovered some biscuits and slipped them on a plate. They settled at either end of the kitchen table.

'My name is Valerie, by the way. I'm Huw's third wife. Or possibly his fourth. We were never quite sure. We only got married three months ago. But we lived together for ages before that.'

He nodded understandingly and tried not to stare. She was so much younger than he expected. Dark good looks that were likely to sharpen. Late thirties maybe. Not negligent of appearance. Merely indifferent. Left to mourn a husband thirty years older. And to question everything.

'So Huw never mentioned El Al. His old partner in crime and colourful adventure?'

'He used to say there were more things he wanted to forget than remember.'

'That sounds just like Huw. Always sharp, incisive.'

The pleasure of recall soon evaporated.

'It seems I must have been one of them. The things he wanted to forget.'

She showed little interest in the echo of battles long ago or the tinge of self-pity in his voice.

'That's one thing I always liked about him,' she said. 'He never lost an inclination to blush. He was never too pleased with himself.'

'You found that attractive?'

He sounded eager to learn.

'He knew how to be ashamed. Not like those egotistical bastards who can't wait to immortalise their ever-so-wicked lives. He never found himself intriguing.'

'That sounds very right.'

He spoke so respectfully they could have sat for any length of time, watching the years fly by as they sat at the table without speaking. The silence of the house closed in and the presence of another person made it easier to bear. In the end he gave a flourish of his hand and the smell of disinfectant wafted through the kitchen.

'So you settled here,' he said. 'Came to rest, so to speak.'

'One of his great-grandfathers was Rector of this parish. So when he heard the Old Rectory was on the market he couldn't wait to buy it. Now I'm lumbered with it.'

He suppressed an urge to move a hand in her direction. It was far too soon to demonstrate any desire to help.

'He was always ridiculously proud of his family. My ancestors he called them. They were people of no consequence really. Farmers and parsons. That sort of thing. But I liked that about him.'

'Ancestor worship,' he said.

'Is that what they call it?'

She was amused. He had created a name for a new category of eccentricity. She straightened her back as though they did not know each other well enough to start being frivolous.

'What was it you fell out about?'

The question was short but precise.

'It's a long story,' he said.

'The end was short enough.'

He paused to consider the tone of her response. It was raw but not bitter. It demanded a frank account.

'I lured him out of the BBC into advertising. He was wasted there. And underpaid. He had all the flair and I knew how to fix things. I made him a partner. He was worth it. It was just the pudding time. The high tide of telly advertising and we caught that tide. We made a lot of money and we were on the way to making more. I flew off to Boston and LA to fix up deals. I wasn't away more than a couple of weeks.

While I was gone he pinched my girlfriend.'

'Oh dear...'

'It may seem a bit childish now but I can tell you I was furious and unforgiving. I wanted revenge. I had to bring him down a peg or two. I cut him out of the deal. And he walked out. It was the end of... well... a real friendship at the very least. I don't think we ever spoke to each other in the old way ever again. Although I longed to. I missed him so much. More than he missed me. I can see that now.'

He closed his eyes, overcome with the cold finality.

'What happened to the girl?'

'Eleri?'

He made a conscious effort of recall as if for a moment the girl's name had escaped him.

'Nothing really. Huw dropped her, she married a minister from Carmarthen. I have a feeling she spent the rest of her life as a language campaigner.'

'She's dead then?'

'I don't really know.'

He realised how lame his answer sounded.

'Huw's friendship meant more to me than Eleri. Anyway I lost them both.'

He waited for some response. There was none forthcoming.

'Not much sound and fury,' he said. 'And precious little significance by now. Except showing up my shortcomings. Of which I am only too aware already.'

He was being weighed up in the silence. He had confessed

enough already. It was a time for a degree of reciprocity. Having come all this way he was entitled to it.

'How did you and Huw meet?'

She smiled.

'He picked me up in a pub.'

He felt obliged to smile as well.

'I was a tormented teacher in a Sec Mod. Bullied by everybody. Exploited too. I went into the pub to cheer myself up. I drank too much to boost my confidence. And he picked me up. You could say Huw Picton rescued me from prostitution. From the classroom anyway.'

'You were very young. And beautiful of course.'

He seemed eager to learn more and eager to please.

'So I clung on to a charming older man. You could say that, yes.'

'Huw was doing well?'

'I knew he was some kind of television executive. It was quite a long time before I realised he was hating every minute of it. He tried for the top job on the Welsh language television channel. "At least there," he said "my time won't be entirely wasted." He didn't get it. I could see he was getting increasingly frustrated. He wanted to write he said. He was trying to write novels. Fine I said. Retire or get yourself sacked or whatever. So off we went. He said we'd rescued each other. He'd rescued me from the classroom and I'd rescued him from television. We were quits.'

'Did he get down to it?'

'We had the whale of a time. Research he called it.'

41

It was time to stem the flow of reminiscence in front of a man she had never met before.

'We settled down eventually. And here we are. Or rather here I am.'

'I'm out of touch with these things,' he said. 'Living in Italy. I do remember he always wanted to write serious stuff. He was wonderfully talented. Are the novels a success?'

'They are wonderful,' she said. 'And unpublished. All five of them. Gathering dust upstairs in what he called his sanctum. He had a big desk in the window and an armchair in which he could sit for hours nursing that beastly Bella and studying the view. I think she can't understand why he's not here. That's why she's behaving so badly.'

'What are they about? The novels.'

He sounded too painfully curious.

'Ancestors,' she said. 'What else. Terribly old-fashioned. Terribly unfashionable. Never mind. He enjoyed writing them and I enjoyed reading them.'

She rose to her feet. The conversation was turning into too much of an interview. It was time to bring the visit to an end. He seemed to be searching for a means to prolong it.

'I would like to pay my last respects,' he said. 'If you could tell me where he's buried.'

'He's not,' she said. 'His ashes are upstairs in the sanctum. Along with masses of papers from his unpublished novels. I've got a war on with the Rural Dean. I want the ashes to go into his grandfather's grave. Or at the foot of it. In a neat casket. The Dean is not keen.'

The visitor sank into his chair. He appeared in desperate need of sympathy.

'I've come too late,' he said. 'For a long time now things haven't gone well. I'd say to myself, I'll look up old Huw. He knows about living. He'll inspire me. And now I've left it too late. It was the best time of my life, with Huw. He had the secret and for a while I shared it. And then I threw it all away. What have I done except grow richer and get more and more empty and lost.'

He looked up at her, his eyes pleading for understanding.

'Is there a Mrs Anwyl?'

Her voice was gentler. She looked at his empty coffee cup as though considering offering him more.

'Alas no. I was too absorbed in making money. And of course I never had anything like Huw's charm whatever the word means. All I know is that it's something I haven't got. Actually I have a partner. Or I had.'

'Oh dear...'

Valerie repeated the comment and then shut her mouth tight in self-rebuke. She held her breath until she saw that he had not noticed the repetition.

'Lucia Caputo. Assistant Curator at the Teodorico. A clever woman. Taught me all I know about tesserae. And a lot more. She got fed up with me. Said I was too rich and too boring. Took a better job in Catania. She wanted to specialise in the mosaics in Sicily. That's why I was down there. Trying to persuade her to come back.'

It seemed a conclusion of a kind. This time she made it

clear it was time for him to leave. At the front door while he stood holding his hat in his hand, still reluctant to go, they were joined by Bella the cat. She rubbed herself ingratiatingly against his trouser leg.

'I admire your garden,' he said politely. 'It's rather big though isn't it?'

She clutched her arms against the breeze from the sea.

'He was always in two minds about the garden. Sometimes he wanted it to run wild and then he would take it in his head to start gardening furiously. In all weathers and at all hours. He said a man had to shelter under a hedge with a crust in his mouth and a sack on his back and mud on his boots to talk to nature. That sort of thing. He was always fun to be with.'

'That sounds real Huw.'

He offered his hand as though they had reached a point of understanding.

'Have you ever been to Italy, Mrs Picton? If you ever feel like a visit I would be more than delighted to welcome you.'

'That's very kind...'

'It's done me so much good, talking to you. I really would like to repay you in kind. Financially I mean. It would give me so much pleasure. I have a villa on Lake Garda. I would be delighted for you to use it. For as long as you like.'

Valerie was shaking her head.

'You said you were lumbered...'

He waved his hat to indicate the size and awkwardness of the Old Rectory.

'I can't leave,' she said. 'Who would feed the cat? He's gone but he may have left the most interesting part of him here. I've got to find out. Huw used to say when it comes to memories we all like to shuffle our own pack.'

Elwyn Anwyl heaved an appropriate sigh. She thanked him briefly as though he had in fact attended the funeral. She watched him leave and returned to stand by the drawing-room window. Bella was padding behind seeing him off. By the road gate he turned for a last look at the Old Rectory. He saw the woman at the window. She looked as unperturbed as the landscape she was staring at. He raised his hat and disappeared from view.

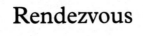

Rendezvous

IN his view an airport was hardly an inspiring setting for a rendezvous, but since it was her decision Henry Davies had no choice. After a good deal of fuss and bother he had arrived with time to spare only to discover her flight from Lisbon was delayed by sixty-five minutes. There was no explanation. It was springtime, the weather was good and there were these European delays and no information. Henry had some expertise in timetables and he was displeased. The condition of the airport was untidy and chaotic with no-one in charge. In the old days, had this been a school, he had only to raise his voice and order would be restored. Now he was brushed aside by a tight bunch of football supporters who charged about bawling their asinine anthems and jostling the multicoloured Asian families all encumbered with children and vast quantities of luggage.

Henry had been tense with anticipation long before arriving and now the tenseness was degenerating into an irritation difficult to contain. He was too well dressed and he fretted about the condition of the flower in his button hole. Would it wilt before Glenys arrived? Should he throw it away? He struggled to dredge up from the depths appropriate quotations with which to bolster his fortitude if not restore his good humour; some rarebit of wit he could repeat when they came face to face after so many, many years. 'Childe Henry to the dark tower came,' for example. He would make regular trips to strategic points such as the electronic arrival boards, bookstalls and toilets to keep his limbs supple and his insides comfortable. Early in his career he had been advised by a cousin who had risen high in the civil service to imagine a wire passing through his spine and out of the top of his head. At times of stress he should give it a good pull to straighten his back or strengthen his walk. The advice had stood him in good stead as he tramped so many miles down school corridors and he continued to bear it in mind as he played nine holes of golf twice a week. There was no par for the course down this anaemic, dreary shopping mall. The effort of being both sprightly and philosophical made him uncomfortably aware of his age. He would be seventy-seven next birthday, and although every-body said he didn't look it, here and now he knew there was no time to lose to add to all the stretches of time that had been lost already.

'Here and now' was a topic he could give his attention to. He found a suitable corner in a café bar up a shallow flight of stairs where he could refresh himself with a well-diluted brandy and soda and rise above the petty irritations that threatened his peace of mind. Throughout his career he had cultivated self-discipline. Always with diligence and what he humorously called his 'fair portion of native cunning' it had been central to his progress, and since his retirement, to his defence against the remorseless advance of the ageing process. He took regular exercise and took care of his health and general appearance.

Was there ever really such a thing as 'now': or was our apprehension of time no more than a sequence of events relative to one another? And as for these events, could they not be atomised or extended ad infinitum according to the emotional and physical condition of the participant masquerading as observer? How better to pass an interlude of inaction than engage in quiet debate. Could the relationship to the balloon glass within reach of his hand be compared to the relationship his hand would enjoy when it clasped the waist of the woman he was waiting for? Glenys. There was still an absurd magic in her name. She was the most momentous thing that ever happened to him. By any measurement, emotional or social, it had to be admitted. To this day. To this expectant hour.

It had been a hazardous love affair that set his life alight; a fire that had smouldered all down the years and was smouldering this very moment. He fingered his balloon glass and saw her in her school uniform, standing in that corner of the school library and smiling at him, drawing him inexorably into her orbit. The school became a palace of enchantment, dangerously exciting. In public view he dared not stand too close to her. She excited him so much. Nothing in his life had been so thrilling, so nerve-racking, as lurking in the organ loft of the parish church while Glenys finished her practising. Then there was the momentous unexpected visit on her bicycle and the passionate embrace outside the back door while his mother was engaged with entertaining the new vicar.

His mother was the problem. And the inordinate pride she had in her only son and in his appointment at thirty-two as the youngest headmaster in the history of the grammar school. A relationship with a girl in the sixth form was out the question. There was no way any regulation or rule could be amended so that the most delicious fruit that life could offer would no longer be forbidden. His mother's hysteria still sent shivers down his spine. It stayed in his mind more firmly than any of the Machiavellian moves he made to keep their unconditional love for each other alive; the devastatingly beautiful young girl pledged herself to the distinguished, but still boyish, youthful older man.

He had been rash enough to take the head boy into his confidence and he had entrusted that bright Liverpudlian spark with the mission of seeing Glenys home from the Christmas dance. It was his anxiety about the length of time the mission took that brought his predicament into the open. His mother insisted that if the secret came out his career would be finished and their lives ruined. He would lose everything they had worked for. Her life would be devastated and so on. Those were awesome weeks when their cherished relationship hung in the balance. In the end, after negotiations in which the vicar and Glenys' family were involved, his mother accepted that they should pay for the two-year course that Glenys would follow in Switzerland, perfecting her French and German and studying music. Her bus driver father could never have afforded it. And after that his mother would relent and they could get married.

But it never turned out like that. How could it! It was an arrangement more suited to the age of antimacassars. The sixties and all their momentous changes had burst upon an immature male of studious nature driven on by the academic ambitions of a demanding mother. In spite of his qualifications and distinguished appearance he was unworldly, still breathlessly naive. Glenys was so much better equipped to deal with it, young, beautiful, charming; too charming to be sent out unprotected into the wider world. She seemed to have had a weakness for older men. First one and then the other, by happy coincidence, were wealthy. At a painfully remote distance he heard about her progress. And whatever piece of news or gossip that reached them his mother seized on to say 'I told you so', or 'you had a lucky escape'. In one way or another she would suggest how grateful he should be for her intervention. It was thanks to her that his career proceeded on an even keel and even when he agreed and showed his gratitude each time they heard something, a part of him would bleed inwardly in silence. All a man of his nature had left was to take solitary walks on the shores of oblivion, stopping from time to time to pick up the pearls of memory when they glittered at his feet.

An unsuccessful marriage to a sports teacher came and

went. In the course of time his mother died. One summer when retirement was already in view he visited Portugal. He took a package tour and stayed at an hotel in Cascais so that he could prowl around Colares in order to smell out the villa that Glenys' second husband, the banker Reinhold von Klopleck, had bought for his retirement retreat. Wearing a new Panama hat, he stood in the small piazza and stared at the gates of the villa. An emaciated dog was stretched out on the stones of the dried fountain, fast asleep. The gates of the forbidden palace were overshadowed by the vast green expanse of an umbrella pine. He returned to the spot more than once, but failed to pluck up the courage to call. He had no wish to meet the rich banker. What he hoped was to bump into Glenys in one of the restaurants in the vicinity, which was both romantic and ridiculous.

On a more practical level, for his retirement he bought a terrace house in Cricieth with the intention of settling on the upper floors and renting the rest to elderly tenants. He found the view of Cardigan Bay quietly inspiring. He passed the time agreeably, playing regular golf, taking field trips with friends, until he heard that the banker von Klopleck had died. The news excited him. He spent time composing a letter of condolence. This gave him an opportunity to initiate a correspondence, cool and friendly to begin with: but calculated to grow more enthusiastic and ardent as time went on. Sensing a degree of sympathy or encouragement, he became more insistent and pleading. Nothing mattered more in the world than to be able to see Glenys again. He was ready to put his life 'back on the market' so to speak and to enter into any arrangement that would bring their lives into closer contact again. He would have her understand that their brief love affair was the best and deepest thing that had ever happened to him. It remained the one glowing torch at the centre of his dull, mundane existence.

'Henry! What on earth are you doing here?'

Inside his new suit he sweated and shuddered like a schoolboy caught in the act. What excuse could he make? What was he going to say?

'Dr H. T. Davies I presume!'

The lighthearted approach was some help. He pushed back his chair and exercised his customary old world courtesy. Always a good line of defence. After all, the woman was a good friend and they had many interests in common. In the past they had exchanged confidences and had been mutually supportive. Mattie Gwilym was inclined to employ a brusque, straightforward manner that was not universally welcomed and she chose to dress with flamboyance not to his taste: but she was stalwart as well as stout, with a devotion to several good causes, she enjoyed a joke and they both shared a keen interest in history and archaeology. They had been on field trips together. On those occasions she had shown an interest in his well-being that veered between the maternal and the flirtatious. She was dressed now in a flouncy black and yellow dress in anticipation of a summer that had not yet arrived and she settled in the seat opposite like a wasp on a choice piece of cake.

'This place is so nerve-racking, I can't tell you!'

Once seated, Mattie had become absorbed in her own flustered condition.

'My granddaughter has been on one of her trips to South America. Research she calls it. Her boyfriend or partner or whatever they call it nowadays, has sworn never to set foot in an aeroplane again. Idiots up there, he says, in search of endless vanity and sensation and weaving a shroud for the planet. He gets quite upset about it. It's a real bone of contention between them and I don't know how it will end.'

She found him slow to appreciate the drama that she could see unfolding. He was smiling in a glazed, polite fashion.

'That's how young people are nowadays. Full of theories. I don't really understand any of it. And in the end I suppose I don't want to. You were a headmaster, Henry. Do you understand it?'

He shook his head soulfully, and wondered how long it might be until her granddaughter's flight was due to land.

'So here I am, a middle-aged go-between. Middle-aged! What am I talking about? Past sixty. When I was a girl that was on the brink of old age!'

Henry struggled to compose a graceful compliment that would reassure Mattie on her robust appearance. There was also the difficulty of how long she would attach herself to him. Was it possible that flights from South America were also delayed?

'And you are meeting somebody?'

His reply was instant: a flash of inspiration.

'A bereaved relative.'

His tone and sepulchral expression implied it would have been indelicately inquisitive for her to inquire further. She showed some concern for his well-being.

'Are you still perched up in that ridiculous top floor flat?'

He smiled and raised his hand to excuse himself from such self-indulgent folly.

'Don't tell me! I'm not getting any younger. I'm thinking of moving. Really. I have it firmly in mind.'

'Good. I tell you what...'

She clasped her plump hands together and leaned closer over the table.

'Awelon y Môr.'

She gave the name as if it was confidential information.

'Brilliant idea. Garden cottages connected up by covered ways with a central block with a restaurant and a club room and all that sort of thing. You still play bridge don't you?'

'As badly as ever,' he said.

'Nonsense. You were jolly good. They've got a keen bridge club there. Then there's golf virtually round the corner. And I don't live so far away, if that doesn't put you off! I think there may be one going vacant next month. Would you like me to put your name down?'

His mouth hung open as he attempted to frame a suitable reply. Mattie was quick to respond.

'You're not keen,' she said.

'It's not that...'

'You're a bit of a Fabius Maximus, aren't you?' she said. 'Delay and all that. Never do today what you can possibly put off till tomorrow.'

This was an old joke between them: and they had their interest in ancient history in common. He smiled and nodded and she took it as an invitation to greater frankness.

'It's a wonderful view and all that but I remember you saying the people downstairs were beginning to get on your nerves. And wasn't there some talk of them taking in refugees..?'

An unintelligible blare on the airport speaker systems caused her sudden alarm.

'Oh, my God... what time is it?'

She began to rummage in her large handbag looking for her spectacles and a small notebook. She scribbled the address of the Awelon y Môr complex with her own telephone number before tearing it out and handing it to him.

'You are just the type they would welcome with open arms,' she said. 'Let's keep in touch. I've got to fly.'

'Of course, Mattie. Of course.'

No longer under surveillance, he was ready to be effusively cordial. He folded the paper, showing gratitude, and stored it in his waistcoat pocket. They waved at each other as she made cautious haste from the sheltered area where they had been sitting. He watched her disappear in the crowded concourse and somehow the world became alive with new possibilities. Anything could happen outside the discipline of inward debates. The most romantic reveries could be transformed into acceptable reality. Here he was, unencumbered and free to comply with anything Glenys suggested. It might even be that she was still inclined to please him. Not as in the old days of course. That was long ago. But there was time left for a new beginning.

He conjured up the delightful images of the young girl that had lived with him so long. He saw her being sculpted gradually by the gentle hand of time: decade by decade growing old gracefully. And what would she be now? An athletic figure, he was confident of that, in her sixties, with some grey hair perhaps but still that same enchanting smile. That could hardly change, anymore than that distant voice on the telephone that had briefly enthralled and thrilled him. 'You sound exactly the same,' he blustered out with boyish enthusiasm. He could have gone on at length but it was only a brief call.

What would they do? What steps would they take to achieve a new way of life, inspired perhaps by the joy they once had in each other? He felt like a man prepared to grapple with the future and take it in his arms. He could move lock, stock and barrel to Portugal, or Glenys could return to Wales. They could share a home together anywhere in the world she fancied. Money was no problem. There were no ties. Everything in the new order would flow from the magic of their being together.

Daydreams are not subject to timetables. The time that he feared would be tedious had flown past. He needed to hasten to arrivals and occupy a conspicuous position at the barrier so that she could catch sight of him as soon as she emerged. He breathed fresh life into the red carnation. He was confident she would recognise him. The flower in his button hole was a gesture of celebration.

The flow of late arrivals began. Some of them looked like survivors who were eager to start living again. Late as they were, there remained a plentiful supply of nearest and dearest waiting to greet them. Celebrations and reunions were in the air. It was a woman in a wheelchair who was the first to recognise him. The airport vehicle in which she sat was being steered by a young woman with a pale face, jet black hair and thick eyebrows. The woman in the chair looked cheerful enough and was pointing at him. It was only when they were close that he realised he was being confronted by Glenys.

'I would have known you anywhere,' she said. 'I bet people keep on telling you you haven't changed a bit.'

Her hand when he clasped it was thin and cold. He wondered whether he should kiss her on the cheek; and who was the younger woman.

'This is Monique,' Glenys said. 'She's a Berber. She doesn't speak much English. And not a word of Welsh.'

Glenys stood up and took hold of Henry's arm while Monique disposed of the chair.

'Monique is wonderful,' she said. 'She smokes like a chimney, and I'm the one that's got cancer. And I've never smoked in my life. There you are. One more of life's little ironies. Where can we get a decent bite to eat? Such a shame that damn plane was late. We won't have much time to talk.'

However little English the Berber woman spoke, she knew her way about airports. She found a lift, which transported them to a lounge which Henry had known nothing about, and within minutes they were ensconced in comfortable armchairs able to gaze at a variety of dormant aircraft through a large window. The best Henry could manage was a confused smile. He failed to say how wonderful it was to see her again. He was slow even to muster up the courage to look at Glenys closely enough to register this change in her appearance. Her skin was mottled with too much sun and her head had lost any feminine aura. With her hair cut short and dyed brown, it looked stern and severe. It made him uncomfortably aware of his own shortcomings even though she was smiling at him. Her lips were thinner but her voice was mercifully the same and he clung to that. Her voice after all was the source of a haunting music he had heard all his life.

'This cancer... '

At last he managed to address the subject.

'Don't worry, Henry. They say it's curable. We shall have to see. At least I can eat cream cakes.'

Monique had laid the tempting plate before them and she was smiling her approval as she sipped her coffee.

'I don't know how long we've got,' Glenys said. 'We are in transit.'

'In transit?'

He heard the dull simplicity in his voice as he repeated the phrase.

61

'To Switzerland. For treatment. I don't know how long we've got. To live I mean. How old are you now Henry?'

'I'll be seventy-seven next birthday.'

'Of course you will. And I'd bet you'll live to be a hundred. You are just the type.'

She smiled as she said it.

'In any case I had to see you. And I've brought you a present.'

Monique opened the briefcase she was carrying and handed Glenys her cheque book. Glenys tore out a cheque already made out to Dr Henry Davies.

'There you are, Henry dear. All the money I owe you for my education. Plus a bit extra for Christmas.'

Henry looked humbled and confused. Glenys had always been cheery and cheerful. Always a breath of fresh air and the spirit of youth and freedom. Life-giving in fact. But this was different. How could he adjust himself to her humour?

'Go on then,' she said. 'Take it. Call it the bride price or whatever. We came all this way to give it to you. And look at you once again.'

He glanced down at the cheque in his hand. It was for a hundred thousand pounds.

'I couldn't possibly...'

'Of course you can. Take it. I've got more than I'll ever need. Think of it as the cost of my education in Switzerland.'

'But you paid that back.'

He sounded cross as he said it.

'My mother said you paid it all back.'

'And did she tell you she also paid for my abortion? A cunning old woman your mother. God rest her soul.'

'An abortion? But we never...'

'Fucked you mean. You were always such a straight-laced romantic. Poor old Henry. At this late stage at least we can afford to be honest.'

Henry closed his eyes. Her voice was relentless.

'No. The culprit was your favourite. The head boy. Gwyn Alun. He said you made me ripe for the plucking. He was a cheeky bastard. He assured me it was perfectly safe. I was fool enough to believe him. I was always incurably curious. And of course it was nothing like it was cracked up to be. And the pill was in its infancy if that is the appropriate expression.'

She was much amused. Monique was paying her the closest attention, whether she understood what was being said or not. Her dark eyes showed concern for Glenys' condition.

'You take that cheque Henry and don't you dare tear it up after I've come all this way to give it to you. Footballers earn that in a week. If you don't want it, give it to some worthy Welsh cause or other. As I remember there were always an awful lot of them.'

Monique murmured Glenys' name. It sounded like an incantation.

'She thinks it's time for us to leave. She knows about these things. She's an absolute wizard at finding her way in this wicked world. Berber blood no doubt.'

Glenys was laughing again. Henry looked so defenceless and aghast.

'We'd better get moving.'

'Let me come with you!'

Henry had reached a sudden decision and was pleading with her.

'Let me come with you. Look after you. Be with you. That's all I ask.'

'Dear Henry. A romantic to the very end. You can come and see us off if you like. But we've had enough of men, haven't we Monique? Life is so much more comfortable without them. Don't take that personally. You were one of the best. Handsome and so well behaved. From here on we do without men. Isn't that right, Monique?'

Much saddened and subdued Henry accompanied the wheelchair to the boarding gate. Glenys made another joke about returning to Switzerland for further education and medication. Henry was unable to smile. Was reality so harsh and rough edged that a man was driven to take refuge in illusions and daydreams and wishful thinking? Was he obliged to cope with this bitter situation on his own? As they passed out of sight, his fingers strayed to the folded piece of paper in his waistcoat pocket.

The Comet

THE first thing that happened was the fax. This was in the days before you could 'kiss your fax goodbye'. In a modest finca on a rocky northern slope of the enchanted island, where tourists were least likely to wander, the fax machine was the acme of modernity, the link with the outside world. Hefin had taken the dogs down the pine forest for one of his inspirational walks. There was the black mongrel bitch, Lollie, long past her reproductive stage but still very lively. Hefin called her the flying hearth rug. And there was Larry, the large amiable husky whose one weakness was chasing sheep. Gisella was hard at work translating the second volume of a history of the American Civil War when the fax machine gave its warning clatter. It could have been from an impatient publisher in Milan. Instead it was from Hefin's father.

Arriving tomorrow at the airport approx 3pm. Flight 507. Sorry for the short notice. Please meet. Bryn Tanat.

Gisella was so dazed and confused she could no longer sit at her desk. Should she run down the rough track to the woods to warn him? That would be silly. She wandered around the whitewashed finca worrying about how her partner would react to the news. Hefin was so sensitive. Gifted, handsome and sensitive. Those were the epithets she regularly attached to the man she shared a life with, just as devoted to his talent as she was to his well-being. He was, as she was ready to point out, spoilt for choice. He painted, he sculpted, he wrote poetry, and he was brilliant at domestic architecture. The question had been, for some years now, on which of these talents should he concentrate? He was only intermittently possessed with the desire to excel. Most of the time he was repelled by the demands of commercialism, the need for publicity, the backbiting that littered these fields of endeavour like mythic crops of dragons' teeth.

Here on their remote slope of this enchanting Balearic island they were at least at peace and reasonably happy. Gisella's industry supported their almost idyllic existence in this picturesque and primitive finca. Hefin could wake up with the rosy fingered dawn breaking over the wine dark sea just as it had done in Homer's day. She was happy to believe that her labours poured showers of miraculous mornings into his lap. Hefin was her handsome agent of perception prepared to transmute the experience into living art. Time would decide into which medium and where the highest results would be achieved.

The awful thing was that Hefin couldn't stand his father. Gisella struggled to understand but she couldn't help feeling that it was something that made life more difficult than perhaps it really needed to be. Of course she was prepared to make sacrifices for the sake of her agent of rare perception: but his father had called him a tinkling cymbal and that was a contemptuous dismissal that was hard for a sensitive soul like Hefin to bear. It took him some time to respond with, 'What does he think he is anyway? Just a sounding brass!' which was near enough, since in those days Bryn Tanat was a prominent member of Parliament renowned for his eloquence. 'A poor man's Aneurin Bevan,' Hefin called his father: which was less offensive than many of the things he chose to say about him.

Two years ago Hefin had returned to the island from his mother's funeral full of bitterness and loathing for his father. 'He destroyed her,' he said. 'That self-absorbed monster destroyed her.' He had picked up a rumour that Bryn Tanat had met up with a rich widow and was planning to marry her after a decent interval. This enraged him further. 'He's a swine,' Hefin said. 'He treated my mother like a slave. I never want to see him again.' Hefin had been very attached to his mother. He said he had been sent away to school by his pitiless father to prevent his mother spoiling him. That rankled all his life and who could blame him? He had worked on an elegiac sequence in her memory for some time, until he had to abandon it to undertake designing a studio for Gustavo and Ernst, a pair of artists who lived in a large wooden chalet four miles away. They were part owners of a fish restaurant in the picturesque creek above Calle san Miguel.

Hearing Hefin's footsteps she went out and kneeled to pet old Lollie. She held up the fax for Hefin to read.

'I can't bear it.'

He crushed the flimsy paper in his hand.

'What does he want to come here for? For what?'

Gisella busied herself pouring water into separate dishes for the dogs. Her head was bent watching them quenching their thirst. She only seemed to half hear Hefin's petulant complaints.

'Just to disrupt things, that's what. Destroy my concentration. Destroy me, really. That's what it's all about.'

She could have said, 'He's your father, Hefin, after all!' but she didn't. Not because she didn't dare but because she had so much work to do. Time would be lost in fruitless recrimination. There was a deadline to meet. She needed to retire behind her texts and her dictionaries and her lexicons. The less she said the better.

'I don't want to see the old bastard, I just don't and that's the end of it. I'll have to get away.'

How could he? They had just enough money to pay the rent and the month's grocery bill. She kept her head down so that he couldn't glare at her as though it were all her fault. Of course in one sense it was. It was her encouragement and her determination and her industry that created the situation here and maintained it. Perhaps her silence would begin to make him realise that much?

'I'm going to see Gustavo and Ernst,' he said. 'It's time we started on the extension at the restaurant. I'm going to walk. I'm not taking the dogs.'

It was a relief to Gisella to see him go. He could walk off

his fury and she could concentrate on yet another chapter of the American Civil War. Translating was a great comfort. Or would be if it was better paid. Some kind of a shelter from the invoices and vicissitudes of their precarious hold on what should have been an idyllic existence. Hefin after all was so gifted and so handsome. On the rare occasions when he deigned to do a bit of shopping, the women on either side of the counter would regard him with an awe and admiration that still gave her pleasure, even when she heard them wonder how he had worn so well when she looked so small and shrunken and worn out. There was a marmoreal quality to her Hefin's beauty and perhaps a certain restraint that could be interpreted as coldness. He had never been as ardent as she felt herself to be. He had a way of being frank and straightforward that suggested a disregard for her feelings; and yet he could say what he liked and had never loosened the grip of her affection. She could be hurt and still turn the sting into something close to an erotic thrill. It was strange, but she knew it was true.

Hefin returned from his trip to the chalet far sooner than she expected. He flung himself down on the wickerwork settee, tired out after the long tramp over hill and down dale.

'Gustavo's gone and done a bunk again,' he said.

'Oh, poor Ernst…'

Her sympathy was instant and heartfelt. Ernst was the quiet, introvert, hardworking Swede. Gustavo the colourful, guitar-playing South American: large, full of fun, easily bored. Hefin displayed an ironic attitude. This was just one more example of human folly and weakness among even the most sophisticated and cultivated people. Gisella was eager for more detail.

'I don't know,' Hefin said. 'Apparently he just jumped up and said: "To hell with it, I'm not going to spend my evenings watching bloody television!" and off he went. He'd taken a fancy to a young Albanian lad working in a bar down in San Antonio. Off he goes like a randy stag!'

'Really,' Gisella said. 'A man of his age. Pushing sixty surely. Poor Ernst will be devastated.'

'Gloomy as hell. Suicidal. Couldn't get a word out of him. Is there anything to eat?'

★★★

Within minutes of the time to start out for the island's only airport, Hefin struck his head against a low lintel and lay moaning on the stone floor. His head was bleeding and he claimed he couldn't see properly. Double vision. So how could he drive? Gisella had to bind his head and then rush to the battered green van they used for journeys into the wider world. It did occur to her as she steered her way down the rock-strewn path that there could be such a phenomenon as accidentally-on-purpose. It could be part of the mechanism of the male of the species and account for many of the vagaries of the historical process. If there was any lesson to be learnt from the American Civil War it had to be how an accidental spark could ignite a conflagration. Even our

72

stumbles are beyond our understanding. It was something that dear Hefin could consider next time his brush slipped when he was painting. Only a thin membrane between accident and inspiration.

Having driven as fast as her nerves could stand, Gisella discovered Bryn Tanat standing in the shade of a palm tree across the road leading to the airport. Even at a distance he was a formidable figure and out of place. In his long overcoat and hat with his luggage at his feet he looked a person of authority at a loss for someone on whom to exert it. Gisella believed she had always been disapproved of, particularly when his wife was alive. She was the evil influence that had led their son astray. For Hefin's sake, Gisella had stiffened her resolve to rise above, or at least ignore, the censure of his family. Bryn Tanat viewed the dust-covered van with distaste and disapproval.

'Is that the best you can manage?' he said.

Gisella's explanations were embarrassed and mumbled. Bryn Tanat looked like a man committed to his own convenience and comfort. He was sweating in his clothes and he wanted to hire a car immediately. This proved more difficult than he expected. It involved a long wait he was not prepared to put up with. He allowed himself to sit in the shade of the van's lumpy passenger seat. He was still the large and handsome bulk of a man, assured of his own importance, that she remembered. He made himself as comfortable as he could and gazed morosely through the dirty windscreen at the sunlit landscape. Gisella nervously pointed out landmarks of interest, turrets and churches, but he was clearly not in a receptive mood.

'What's he got against me?'

The first time Gisella failed to hear the question above the noise of the engine, so he repeated it. His eyes were staring at her, large and liquid, to show he was a father, hurt, injured. Her mouth opened, her neat head shook as she groped around for an appropriate answer. She couldn't issue an outright denial of what they both knew was only too true.

'You are a bit overwhelming.'

It was the best she could come up with. She freed a hand from the steering wheel to make a gesture that after all she was expressing herself in a second language.

'Am I?'

To her surprise he looked rather pleased. This enabled her to smile and she knew her smile was considered her most attractive feature.

'Well, I only wanted the best for him. Always.'

That had to be true. The problem was how you defined 'good', and what was the distinction between 'better' and 'best'? Plainly the son inherited self-will from the father as well as masculine good looks. Could it be possible that despising success could be as damaging as desiring it? Inspired by Bryn Tanat's presence she was quietly excited to speculate.

'I could have been wrong of course.'

It was a substantial admission for a professional politician to make. She was struck with the elegiac tone with which he made it. Something could have brought about a change of heart. But could it? In a man of his age. She covered her own confusion by apologising for the roughness of the track they were beginning to climb. He was barely listening.

'They've shoved me out of the shadow cabinet.'

He was almost talking to himself, yet he wanted her to hear.

'So I'll never hold office.'

He expected her to sympathise.

'This New Labour lot. All they want is power. Don't give a damn about socialism.'

She wondered how much she cared. She had to remind herself she was a Swiss citizen from the Ticino. She had convictions but they weren't political. Or were they? Perhaps everything connected with Hefin and his father was political in the end. It made the prospect different and disturbing.

'They're going to win. That's all that matters. That's what it's all about.'

He turned to address her directly.

'Is that why you've settled out here? Out of the rat race as they call it?'

He was making a visible effort to understand. There was no simple answer she could give him. She could say how little she understood British parliamentary practice, or that politics in general were something his son had little time for. He was concentrating on expression and perception in depth, transmuted into artistic forms. That would irritate him.

Hefin's standard view was that finance power controlled everything in the world and they lived here to be least subjected to it.

'I miss Morfudd so much. My days are so empty without her.'

He gave a deep sigh. He was still grieving. After two years. Gisella had to accept it.

'She was a real socialist. Ready to make sacrifices. Her mother had had to stand in a queue to wait her turn at the soup kitchen in the Rhondda. That was something they never forgot. Lined up like starving cattle. We were determined that nothing like that should happen again. She was dedicated. Really dedicated. That's why we sent Hefin away to school. So we could give all our time to the cause. We worked our guts out. As she saw it my career and the cause became one. And now they're both gone.'

That rumour about a rich widow? It had to be a lie. Or maybe they had fallen out? At second hand, from her experience of translating the memoirs of politicians, they were capable of anything in order to justify themselves. At least Hefin's father was trying to be honest.

'What's done is done. You can't go back and undo it.'

This seemed a truth to which they could both subscribe. You just had to soldier on and make the best of it. Towards the end of the journey Gisella warmed towards him. It was possible the father's visit would not be so dire after all.

On the bare ground outside the cactus hedge in front of their finca, Gisella was astonished to see parked a gleaming new four by four she had never seen before. Bryn Tanat pointed at it.

'That's the kind of vehicle you need around here. It's not yours, is it?'

Gisella shook her head, obviously puzzled.

'I'll have to get you one.'

He emerged to admire the compact machine. In these primeval surroundings it could have been an object dropped from outer space. Gisella hurried into the house. Out of the gloom of the interior she was greeted by a loudly cheerful Home Counties voice.

'Gisella! I was about to seduce your lovely husband! Doesn't he look romantic with a bandage around his head!'

Alison Loomis was holding up both her hands as though caught in the act. Alison was a leading figure in their circle. Cheerfully divorced from a rich American banker, she had built for herself a house in the Moorish style with cloisters and flat roofs and a landscape garden where it gave her much pleasure to entertain her artistic friends. Gisella and Hefin were particular favourites because they were ready to help in the garden.

'The thing is my dear, we've got to do something about Gustavo. He's very naughty. We can't have him behaving like this. Breaking poor Ernst's heart.'

Gisella nodded nervously. Hearing voices, Bryn Tanat was lingering outside.

'What I thought was, we could go down there in my new jalopy and root him out. He's such a naughty boy!'

'I hope you're not talking about me!'

Bryn Tanat crossed the threshold as though the loud voice he heard was an invitation to a public occasion. He was no longer morose or despondent. If there was a bit of liveliness going on he was very ready to join in. Nervously Gisella made the introductions.

'Alison. This is Hefin's father. Bryn Tanat. Member of Parliament.'

'My goodness. We are honoured.'

There was a competition in loud laughter as they shook hands.

They were instant kindred souls: a cheerful man in his late sixties and a redoubtable woman not much younger. Gisella's accent and apprehensive manner had made the introduction sound charmingly quaint.

'Now we can see where the boy's good looks came from!'

Bryn Tanat was resolved to be positive and modest.

'He's got more than that,' he said. 'I'm only a politician. He could be something much more if he chose to be.'

Hefin's response was to lurk further behind Alison Loomis, his bandage white and discouraging in the deeper gloom.

'Look, I mustn't keep you,' Alison said briskly. 'I intrude on a family reunion.'

Bryn Tanat managed to show concern for his son's bandaged head. The damage gave Hefin an excuse for a lack of enthusiasm. Their encounter was muted, but already acquiring tension.

'So I'm off,' Alison said. 'So nice to meet you. Look, all of you. I'm planning a little roof party on Friday evening. To say hello to that famous comet with a funny name. It also happens to be my birthday, but you can ignore that. I do hope you'll come. And Mr Tanat! I would love to show off a nice new face. Expats tend to see too much of each other. Now I'm off to frogmarch the naughty Gustavo home.'

Hefin became suddenly animated. He followed Alison into the open air.

'You can't go into that nasty hole alone, Alison. I'm coming with you.'

He went back indoors.

'Look I'll be back in a couple of hours. Well in time for supper. We can't possibly let her venture into that bar alone. It's a ghastly place. Anything could happen. Gisella, you explain to my father. I'll be back in no time.'

***

The dogs took to Bryn Tanat and he took to them. Their sense of smell seemed to tell them there was a generic relationship between the men who took them to run in the pine forest. They responded to the same note of encouragement and reprimand. Bryn Tanat was happy to attribute their good behaviour to the authority he had with animals in general. 'At least they do as I say,' he would say. 'Which is more than I can say for the higher species. If they are higher.' The tranquil remoteness in this north corner of the island encouraged him to philosophise and Gisella was an experienced listener. He took some interest in her work and knew quite a lot about the American Civil War. When he questioned her too closely Gisella had to confess it was the language she was concerned with more than the content. She was quick to add that his knowledge had given her labours a new interest.

Hefin returned in triumph. Together he and Alison had plunged into the darkest corner of the lion's den and plucked out Gustavo from the corner where he was feeding his Albanian boy with a giant ice cream. They sent the boy packing and Gustavo was now lodged in Alison's Moorish palace and being given a good talking to – 'debriefed' Hefin called it – before being reunited with his loved one. When Gisella filled in the background for Bryn Tanat, Hefin's father pulled a face expressing his repulsion. The son could not forebear to comment.

'What's this? A slight attack of homophobia?'

'Is that what they call it? I suppose I'm old fashioned. Let's say it doesn't agree with me.'

Gisella did her best to explain that normally Gustavo and Ernst were a sweet and loving couple. In the interests of harmony, Bryn Tanat said 'If you say so' and tried to make it clear he was here to learn and understand. It was a display of modest restraint that left Hefin increasingly suspicious. The crucial moment came at the end of a quiet supper.

'You know why I've come, don't you?'

Gisella grew tense as she waited for Hefin's response. It was possible he could say something outrageous, like 'to disturb my peace. What else?' Instead her hero looked mildly ridiculous. The bandage around his head was working loose and his mouth was open with no sound emerging.

'I want you to design a house for me.'

It was as much a chairman of a committee awarding a commission as a warm paternal smile. Hefin raised two hands to his bandage and frowned as if his head had begun to ache.

'I inherited a smallholding above Aberaeron. I think I told you. And I have planning permission which is a major achievement in that neck of the woods, I can tell you.'

Gisella could sense it was a mild political joke. She did not venture to ask for more explanation.

'Fantastic view. You can see all the way from Tŷ Ddewi to Ynys Enlli. What more can a man ask for in this world?'

He made a generous gesture.

'A complete free hand. What more could an architect wish for? Something new. Something to get your teeth into. Something important.'

Gisella held her breath, poised to rejoice and even clap her hands. She had detected a note of appeal. This was a peace offering as well as a challenge. Surely something to be welcomed with open arms? There was a tense silence while they waited for Hefin's response. He was in no hurry. His position strengthened the longer they had to wait.

'It's a great idea.'

The tone was quiet and neutral and no more, but it allowed Gisella to relax a little and smile.

'The trouble is I've got a pile of commitments. I'm working on an extension to Gustavo and Ernst's restaurant and a plan for a studio. And there's Gertrude Tibbot's studio unfinished. If I don't turn up on site virtually every day the craftsmen just wander off on another job. They never finish anything if they can help it. Mañana. Never in any hurry.'

'Yes, well, when you've got your brains back, think it over. I'm not in any hurry either.'

★★★

Within a day or two Bryn Tanat had made himself very much at home. He managed to hire a four by four and took an interest in the history of the island. Most of the time he was in high good humour. He even apologised for being a cuckoo in the nest and added that it was just as well there were no chicks around that he would have to kick out. He was not too concerned about his son's lack of response or Gisella's slowness to catch on to his more colloquial efforts. He found Alison Loomis delightfully quick on the uptake. He paid a visit to her garden and demonstrated that in spite of his age he was just as willing as his son to lend a hand and was far more appreciative of the range of flowering shrubs and variety of fruit trees and the general beauty of the landscape.

Most mornings Bryn Tanat arose early. Gisella would find him sitting on the narrow terrace under the wisteria admiring the sunlight creeping along the water offshore changing

82

its colour and the light and shade on the rocks. She brought him coffee and French bread and honey and he burbled something about a 'lordly dish' and declared it was all something he could very easily get used to.

His father's conspicuous content drove Hefin to an unaccustomed fury of activity. There seemed to be a hundred-and-one things demanding his instant attention. Gisella had to be pleased to see so many projects edging closer to completion. Her own work was able to proceed because Bryn Tanat insisted she should not allow his presence to distract her. He went shopping as if it were a great adventure and bought ready-made meals and bottles of wine. He continued to take the dogs for their runs into the pine forest and down to the cove where they could scramble happily over the rocks. The thing he liked about dogs he said was they treated each day as though it had never happened before. And he was feeling a bit like that himself.

'You can see what he's up to, can't you?'

Hefin seized a chance to demand Gisella's close attention. He leaned over her as she concentrated on her translating. He spoke in a harsh whisper although there was no-one else within earshot. Gisella was unnerved by the intensity in his voice. It was something she had hoped not to hear. There had been a measured distance between father and son but a level of politeness. Within the limits of his boisterous nature, the parliamentarian was doing his best to please. Given time she had hoped for the possibility of a growing closer, a reconciliation even. It had been comforting for her to work on that assumption; at the very least to make the visit bearable; a stepping stone to better things.

'It's second nature to him. He always uses people. Especially women. Get the female vote, he used to say, and then you're halfway there. He's trying to get at me through you. Don't you see it?'

She sighed deeply.

'Don't you think he's changed, Hefin? A changed man, I mean.'

'Politicians don't change. That's why we live out here, for God's sake. Self-willing egotistical bullies with elephant skins pretending they know how to run the world. Remember that bunch of them at the Tait-Willis party in South Ken? Bryn Tanat strutting about full of his own importance. In or out of office, all busy feathering their own nests. Don't you remember?'

She remembered very well. It was the turning point in their lives. Hers particularly. A moment like a religious conversion. It was from that very party they made their escape together. She abandoned her natural Swiss caution, her meticulous research work, her metropolitan opportunities and threw in her lot with this handsome young artist of simmering rebellion and infinite promise. Escaping they believed from his father's clutches and treadmill in search of a higher destiny. He was making an appeal to history, their history. He needed her. Her support. Her loyalty.

'He has really changed.' She ventured to speak with a little more authority. 'Politics don't appeal to him any more. He

84

told me they tried to shunt him off to the House of Lords. He said he wasn't having any of it. The House of Lords is obsolete he said. Most of the system was out of date and useless. That's what he said.'

'Did he?'

'Oh yes. That's what he said.'

'And did he tell you how many companies he has joined as a non-executive director? The great socialist accumulating capital. Did he tell you that? He's playing you like a little fish at the end of a line.'

'I'm not quite so stupid, Hefin. Designing a house in a landscape, this is something you've always wanted. You've said so. In every detail. From start to finish.'

'You can't see any further than your nose. All the strings attached and you can't see them.'

'At least it's worth thinking about. Less financial pressure. Less worrying about money.'

'Ah! So that's it!'

'A little more freedom, Hefin. A breathing space.'

'What a temptation… let me spell it out for you. I build the house and he lives in it and you live there as his housekeeper and nurse. He's making an insurance policy for his old age. Manipulating every inch of the way. And you can't see it.'

'Suppose that is true. The need for protection and comfort in old age is a human frailty not a fault.'

She turned abruptly back to her work. That left him crosser than ever. He stamped out of the house fuming.

***

A gap had opened between them that had never existed before. Gisella had always been aware of an irrational element in Hefin's nature. She had believed it was necessary to the creative process. Now, all it seemed to be doing was fuelling his hatred for his father and she found this deeply troubling. He couldn't even bear to see Bryn Tanat enjoying himself. At the party the newcomer was a centre of attention. When there were people to listen to him, he could always find something striking to say.

'What I like about their way of life is, it's down to essentials. I like that.'

He was talking to Frank Wilmot, an asthmatic London publisher who made his home on the island and gardened in friendly competition with their hostess. Dr Ortega, the local physician, was also listening and his wife Magda, a physiotherapist who treated Alison's arthritis.

'Modern life has too many frills attached to it. Especially in capital cities. They set the tone. It's all instant gratification. It can't go on. The planet can't sustain this degree of exploitation and people have to learn to live on less. But will they? There's the rub.'

As if to console himself Hefin had been drinking more than usual. Gisella trembled when she heard his voice in her ear. There was no knowing what he would say.

'Pontificating remind you of something? South Ken

redivivus. He'll form a government one way or another. And we'll be attendant lords and servants. You can't see it, because you don't want to.'

His father was threatening to steal the close attention and constant care his delicate talent needed. He was turning against her because he had no other target. And yet her heart bled for him. Their way of life depended on her love. She could not dare to be disillusioned. She made her way through the library to the short flight of steps that led to the roof garden. She knew she would find Ernst there, sitting alone on the parapet edge and gazing at the constellations. The stars all seemed so close, glittering powerfully through the unpolluted air. The comet was due to arrive above the horizon. Gisella sat close to Ernst and took his hand.

'They seem so close,' he said. 'They could be looking down with interest. But they're not. Why should they?'

From indoors they heard singing. Gustavo was accompanying himself on the guitar. People stopped talking to listen. His warm baritone was a melting sound in the quiet evening air.

'He's written a song for Alison's birthday,' Ernst said. 'He's such a child really. He's never grown up.'

Gisella murmured 'Ernst' and squeezed his hand. They were fellow sufferers from the same strange complaint. How long was an infatuation supposed to last? They wanted to go on deceiving themselves because it would be intolerable not to. Gustavo stopped singing. There was clapping and laughter and animated conversation was resumed. The volume of sound increased as the wine flowed freely. Ernst and Gisella were alone on the roof, bringing some comfort to each other.

'I don't know why he should be like this. I can feel how distressed he is. What can I do?'

Gisella murmured her question. Ernst's answer was abrupt.

'He's jealous.'

'But there's no reason at all…'

'You hold your ground,' Ernst said. 'I tell you. He's nothing without you.'

In twos and threes the guests began to arrive on the roof and look up at the stars with a sudden solemnity as though they were arriving in a roofless church. Gustavo arrived still strumming his guitar. He was the first to catch sight of the comet as it travelled majestically across the starry sky from the east. As they watched the comet everyone fell silent and subdued, only a dog barking on a distant hillside broke the silence. The comet travelled with such effortless, awesome power, as far away from the earth as the sun, and reducing the size and significance of everything living on the planet, including themselves. Frank Wilmot murmured: 'It's humbling'.

The silence couldn't go on for ever. As soon as people began talking Hefin seized the opportunity to capture their attention. He stood on the parapet. He was swaying dangerously.

'I've written a poem,' he said. 'There's no reason why you shouldn't hear it. You listen to all sorts of rubbish.'

Gisella raised her arm to restrain him. Her mouth opened

but no sound came out. Whatever she said would only agitate him further.

'Visitor from Heaven's Gate! You bear a message and I can hear it. When you return in four thousand years there will be no-one here to see you. Not one soul. We will have snuffed ourselves out. The human race will drag down all the beasts and the forests and the flowers with them and all will be dispersed in the solar wind...'

He made one gesture too many, lost his balance and tumbled into the garden below, leaving behind first a stunned silence, and then screams and cries of concern and a stampede from the roof by the shortest way to the garden. They found him there, stretched out and moaning. Dr Ortega took charge. He prevented Gisella from taking the prone figure in her arms.

'Don't move him,' he said. 'Magda is phoning for an ambulance.'

Bryn Tanat took off his jacket and made a pillow for his son's head. He was murmuring. 'Don't worry, lad. We'll take care of you.'

He looked at Gisella who was kneeling on the other side. 'We'll take care of him, won't we?'

She nodded, her face stiff with the effort of stifling a long wail. There was no telling how bad the fall had been. He just lay, between them, unable to move. He was the only one still looking at the sky. He watched the comet sail on its predestined course, incandescent, and unconcerned.

Luigi

HE counted for nothing. Less than a stray cat. It was cold among the ruined tombs where black cypresses stood stencilled against the violet sky. The Moroccan troops had used the shelled church as a latrine after ransacking the place and pressing on. They didn't bother with the heap of obsolete weapons left in the church. Luigi fingered the hand grenade under his torn cloak and stretched his mouth to try to stop his lower lip from quivering. He was eighteen. Could any of it mean anything? A starving cat crept along the edge of darkness. Yellow eyes. Malevolent reflections of the moon. The war was lost. Would he be better off dead? Dead as his noisy cousin Rodolfo, shot through the mouth while he was singing at the top of his voice standing on a truck in the middle of that Piazzale that was supposed to be deserted. Death and desertion. Death and betrayal. Was that all it amounted to? Was there nobody left to shoot?

'Be your own man, Luigi Perone!'

Awful echo from a vanished world. Uncle Vittorio's exhortations. The old fraud. The old fool.

'Life is an adventure, Luigi. Always be swift and well directed as a torpedo in a stormy sea!'

A short sharp academic sticking his chin out like his hero, and his goatee wagging as he went on chewing up the world into words.

'Be your own man, Luigi. As sharp as steel on a whetstone! Stoke the fire in your heart with bitter memories of all your beloved country's humiliations.'

Whatever Uncle Vittorio chose to say was Holy Writ in his brother's humble abode. Had he not fought and run and fought again on the Piave and been among the first to sense the overwhelming genius of their country's saviour? Uncle Vittorio had achieved the ultimate accolade of a professorial chair. He corresponded with Gentile and Bottai. He lived in a fine house undisturbed by childish caterwauling, and he had roses growing on the terrace, which he loved to water. Luigi was the nephew he chose to single out from his bank-clerk brother's brood, and favour with advice and exhortation and occasional pocket money and talk of conquering a future with a capital F. Luigi was the best looking and, from the conquest of Abyssinia, designated to take part in victory celebrations and wear an assortment of becoming uniforms.

'As Luigi grows, the Empire grows!' said Uncle Vittorio.

His brother was always eager to agree with him. Luigi's mother was proud too. Her boy was a picture. But she was always so apprehensive. Uncle Vittorio attributed that weakness to her peasant origins.

'If the sight of blood upsets you, boy, I recommend you visit the slaughterhouse once a week until you get used to it!'

The goatee wagged and Luigi obeyed. Believe, obey and fight. That's what it all amounted to. Uncle Vittorio seemed privy to Il Duce's innermost thoughts. They had it all worked out. In order to ensure a glorious future they had to revive the Roman Empire in a new streamlined, modern form. To do that they had to conquer the air. And to do that they needed to dare and hold their nerve. Abyssinia was the perfect illustration. Natives could always be bombed into submission. Il Duce made his sons airmen and Uncle Vittorio stuffed Luigi into the air cadets. With reduced railway fares the great man took the entire family to visit the huge 1937 exhibition celebrating the two thousandth anniversary of the birth of the Emperor Augustus. Luigi was growing fast; the uniform he wore was too tight for him and he vomited in the Foro Romano.

'Be bronze, be bold! Build yourself up in his image!'

Be pale. Be sick. Be dead. She wouldn't miss him. Would it be worth going on living to shoot her?

The great pride of his life had been to march at her side in that last triumph. Uncle Vittorio said their photo in the local paper should be made into a Youth at the Helm poster. Luigi Perone and Sylvana Lanzi. The Fascist future. Sylvana was the youngest daughter of Avvocato Lanzi and the Lanzis were the wealthiest family in Castiglione. The town was held together by the alliance between the Avvocato and the Professor. Uncle Vittorio called it a marriage of convenience in his nephew's hearing. In her black uniform Sylvana was style incarnate. She had a pretty bell-like voice, liable to ululate when expressing reproach. This did nothing to deter Luigi. He stole her photograph from the noticeboard of the Casa Balilla and hid it under his mattress along with a colour reproduction of Botticelli's 'Birth of Venus'.

The first impact of the war was the end of celebrations and youth parades. People were encouraged to tighten their belts and stick closer together. That suited Luigi. Increasing co-operation between the Avvocato and the Professor meant he could see Sylvana oftener. War or no war that was more than enough to gladden his heart. The moonlight meant something then. They could sit on the stone bench in the public gardens and she would allow him to hold her hand while she complained about her sisters and the intolerable restrictions of her life at home. Her mother wouldn't allow her to join the Croce Rossa, no matter how becoming she looked in the uniform. 'We have a duty to ourselves,' her mother would say. 'And life should be a stretching experience.' He'd been stretched all right. And now he was stretched out. Already dead inside.

And yet the young could sometimes wear white and play tennis. Uncle Vittorio would glue his ear to the wireless and fulminate and fume about the conduct of the war and curse one incompetent general after another. It was the only time he ever heard his uncle criticise the great leader. 'How is it after every disaster the culprit gets promoted to Field Marshal?' On the loggia of the Villa Lanzi the Professor and the Avvocato would mutter about shortages and vital resources and unite in criticising Count Ciano and his cronies. Uncle Vittorio even went as far as calling them 'corrupt degenerates'. They had to blame somebody. Never themselves.

That summer morning they set out together on their bicycles for the mountains. It was freedom bordering on ecstasy printed forever on his brain. Beyond the vineyards and the orchards and the fragrance of the chestnut forests to a world still green in the sun. Bathing in the mountain stream, and the command in those tinkling tones to move away while she undressed. Glimpses of a white thigh between obedient fingers. Home-baked bread in the saddlebag of his bicycle and his mouth in the stream and Sylvana's rippling reflection in the water like a glimpse of heaven. For the first time she allowed him to nibble her shell-like ear while she murmured her distress about a gallant cousin wounded on the terrible Russian front and now convalescing in a hospital in Senigallia. Would he ever walk again and could she go and visit him, the first love of her life? Intoxicated with devotion, he vowed to get her there. He never did. She allowed him to kiss her chaste lips but resisted the crude thrust of his tongue. After the initial disappointment, it was enough to raise her even higher on her celestial pedestal.

That unforgettable day. The young people's prolonged absence had gone unnoticed. On the loggia the Avvocato and the Professor were locked in heated argument. The world had come to an end and they disagreed violently what to do about it. The enemy had landed in Sicily like a hobnailed boot on an anthill, and the bewildered creatures were already scattering in all directions. The Fascist Grand Council, by a vote of nineteen against six, had put an end to the dictatorship. The King had placed Mussolini under arrest. Uncle Vittorio was tramping up and down the loggia smelling out traitors. 'That Ciano,' he said. 'Didn't I tell you? That Grandi! Fops! Tailor's dummies! Why convene the Grand Council in the first place? Why provoke a crisis?' In spite of nervous agitation and much chewing of his trim moustache, Avvocato Lanzi's response was as ever measured, consciously diplomatic. The situation had to be faced. The king, whatever his short stature and shortcomings, was the king and therefore head of the armed forces. A commander-in-chief commanded an oath of allegiance. At this Uncle Vittorio exploded. His oath of allegiance was to Il Duce, the country's saviour. His eyes rolled in his head with the intensity of his loyalty and he foamed at the mouth. Traitors should be shot. The lot of them. The miserable dwarf of a King first, and then that bungler Badoglio. At this the Avvocato stiffened and he called out as though there were an audience present. 'Viva il re! Viva Italia.' That was the end of their collaboration. As far as he knew, they never spoke to each other again.

In those anxious August days his life was governed by stubborn attempts to keep in touch with Sylvana. The Lanzis owned several remote farms, which in such troubled times, were natural hiding places. There were prisoners of war let loose in the countryside and men from disbanded regiments and heavy German units rumbling south and taking the country over. Uncle Vittorio kept a low profile until Mussolini was rescued by the Germans and then he began to jump up and down again possessed with patriotic fire. 'Not another inch of ground,' he said. 'Not another inch. Festung Europa! Hang on my brave boys until our twin leaders unleash their terrible secret weapon that will bring victory with a capital V.'

So he found himself sitting between his cousin Rodolfo and Mario Crispi singing 'Goodbye, my love, Goodbye', in an open truck driving north, and where were they now? Both dead. His mother's tears streamed down her face when he exchanged his light suit and short-sleeved shirt for the black uniform and badges and his Uncle Vittorio, the old fool, telling her to be proud of her son, and his father shrinking in the shadows. What a world, what a life spinning like a top in ever decreasing circles before it topples over. Always cold. Invisible enemies called partisans shooting out of the dark. A firing squad in a school yard. Blood on the walls. Always cold. Minefields everywhere. Spitfires out of the sky shooting at anything that moved. Mario's legs. Stumps he tried to bind with a belt to stop the bleeding. Never any help when you needed it. He'd seen the bloody saviour. And heard him. A tamed bull with a big cap pulled down over his fat ears and German officers just a few steps behind him. 'Fight well, lads! This is your Italian Social Republic, so defend it! You still believe in me.' And then he left the motley parade of young and old in a hurry.

In the end that was the one thing to do. Leave in a hurry.

Fear governed the world. The squat, fanatical sergeant from Cremona took a particular dislike to Luigi because he carried a hair comb in his tunic. 'You mother-fucking rabbits better be more afraid of me than the enemy. When I shoot deserters, I don't miss.' On his eighteenth birthday he filled his rucksack with rations and slipped away from the hay-loft. He thought then he had something to live for. He had to be resourceful. Moving at night. Sleeping on threshing floors. Stealing bread and salami, and civilian clothes from clothes lines. There was a danger of travelling in circles. And then he came to the woods above the terrace hills of olive groves and vineyards and Castiglione on its familiar hill.

Self-preservation made him creep in the dark like a rat down the alleyway to the back door of his home. The back door his grandmother used to leave open on Christmas Eve in case the Holy Family, fleeing from Herod's soldiers, should need shelter and a bite to eat. There would be a flagon and a loaf on the bare kitchen table. The door was locked. He had to beat it with his tired fists. When at last she recognised his voice there was more fear than relief in her welcome. Her life was out of control. She couldn't say how many days ago Uncle Vittorio had been shot dead by red bandits as he was getting into his car. They had vanished and he was buried, and the English forces occupied the town. There was a man called the Town Major installed in the Municipio, and he had appointed Avvocato Lanzi as provisional Communal Secretary. 'Hide my son. Hide. These are dangerous days. Your father is ill. He has taken to his bed.'

His mother's trembling gave Luigi a fresh access of courage and cunning. Beyond his great-aunt's vineyard there were caves in the rock where the old woman used to keep hens. A dry hiding place in the daytime. At night he could move about. From that heap of abandoned weapons in the ruined church to the edge of the Piazza Cavour. All that was left in the world for him was to see Sylvana and speak to her. In the town there was khaki everywhere and no black to be seen. No Fascists. No Germans. Young partisans from nowhere swaggering around with red scarves around their necks. That was what the world had come to. His first glimpse of Sylvana was entering the Municipio escorted by an officer in khaki. She was as smart as ever in her Croce Rossa uniform. And the officer was most attentive. Most gallant. After dark, Luigi followed her home. She screamed when he placed a hand on her shoulder. 'Luigi. You are still alive?' That was as much welcome as he gained. She urged him to go away. The red partisans were still around. But for the protection of Major Hill there was no knowing what would have happened to her father. Get away as far as you can. He slunk away like a dog that had been kicked.

He was an outcast. That was all it amounted to. Skulking on the outskirts. From the ruined church to the cave in the tuffo where his mother left food she pretended was for the hens. Soon the day came when bells rang out for victory. Whose victory for God's sake? It was the dancing on the piazza that drove him to despair. Lamps lit in the trees. He watched her dancing in that English officer's arms. The red cross on her breast, starched white collar, white stockings, white shoes. As elegant as ever. So gay. So charming. Enslaving another admirer. Giggling out her bits of English and the officer so plainly entranced. And that clanking song on the merry-go-round about the blue sky getting bluer every day.

The moment the officer moved away he grasped her arm and dragged her outside the circle of light. He refused to be sent away. I've got a grenade in my hand under my coat. You come with me or I'll blow us up. He struggled to stop his voice trembling. She was so close. You would never do it. Don't be so sure. You don't know what I've been through. You've no idea. I know you. She was taking charge as she always used to do. Her mesmerising voice. Her scent. You are a nice boy, Luigi. Sympatico. She was touching his cheek with her fingers. You aren't a savage. You are gentle. That's what I always liked about you. Go now. Major Hill is coming back.

And that was it. The hand grenade still under his dirty cloak. Among the cypress trees two cats began to spit and scratch and squabble. He aimed the grenade at them. It failed to go off. Just as obsolete as himself. He shuffled into the filthy church. Through the torn roof the moonlight shone on the altar. He stretched himself on the bare surface to wait for the slate grey light in the sky that would precede a new dawn.

Vennenberg's Ghost

GRIFFITHS, Afforestation, handled the coloured print with a certain disdain. A random record of someone else's night-time revelry had found its way into a wallet of sober views of properties for sale.

'Where on earth did this come from?' he said.

'I suppose I must have taken it. Although I must admit I don't remember doing it.'

Griffiths' companion sitting at the cast-iron terrace table was Marloff, Aridlands. They were colleagues and friends, international civil servants on leave, bound even more closely by their wives being cousins. Marjorie Marloff and Myfanwy Griffiths had gone to bed leaving their husbands to their cigars and brandy and their taste for a pleasant mixture of reminiscence and disputation.

'Never mind. It's quite useful. Gives you some idea of the atmosphere, Griff. This girl on the left could be a key player.'

A night at the Villa Louisa was an agreed break on their journey south. The two childless couples had often enjoyed holidays together and now they were setting out on a pilgrimage to find a suitable property for their retirement due in four or five years' time. Geneva, where Griffiths and Marloff were stationed, had the wrong climate for Marjorie's sciatica. Both she and her husband wanted to settle in the south. Myfanwy was devoted to her cousin and would do most things to please her. Griffiths took up his usual position of needing to be convinced. This need grew stronger when his wife was not present to accuse him of being obstructive or unconstructive. He had the larger share of disposable capital and, like an amiable bank manager, he was prepared to sit back in his chair and listen. He also enjoyed an argument. No holds barred.

'It's too easy,' he said.

'What is?'

'Superficial conviviality. Typical.'

They squinted at the photograph in turn.

'Who is this priapic creature in the middle?'

'That's Mario. As you can see a cheerful soul.'

Mario was awarding the camera a faunlike possessive grin: a force of nature with close-cropped hair, narrow eyes and a bull neck thrust forever forward.

'He looks the apotheosis of greed to me,' Griffiths said. 'I wouldn't trust him any further than I could throw him.'

'That wouldn't be far.'

This was a frank reference to Griffiths' plump condition. Marloff made more of an effort to keep himself in shape. He still played tennis and squash. Griffiths smoked cheap cigars and the most physical effort he was inclined to make was a brief swim and a prolonged sunbathe when the weather permitted.

'And the woman in question?' Griffiths said. 'This one.'

The woman on Mario's right had long fair hair and a smile that seemed to bleed down a pretty confused face.

'The fair Annette. Annette Vennenberg. She owns everything. You may as well say our fate is in her hands.'

'And this one?'

Griffiths wanted to know about the younger woman on Mario's left. Her black hair and her white teeth glittered with acquisitive intention.

'That's Giusi,' Marloff said. 'All the way from Sicily. What a contrast eh? Annette from Augsberg and Giusi from Agrigento. And Mario the mighty determined to serve them both with equal enthusiasm. A joyful symbol of European unity.'

'Huh,' Griffiths grunted. 'More like a testament to the hopelessness of the human condition.'

'Now then,' Marloff said. 'Now then Griff old boy. You're doing it again.'

Marloff was a Swiss of White Russian extraction, but he had been to Cambridge and he liked to indulge in a worldly drawl. He would tease his friend and then tell him not to be so touchy.

'It's your Puritan upbringing,' Marloff said. 'You can't help it.'

'Can't help what?'

'Confusing morals with mores, what else? You deal too much in abstractions, old boy. I mean you just couldn't go telling these people that life is a pilgrimage or whatever. They simply wouldn't understand you.'

Griffiths struck the table with the edge of his hand as if to announce that the debate had started.

'Right and wrong should apply with equal force throughout the planet.' he said. 'They should be universals. Otherwise the distinction is not worth making.'

Marloff's finger was already extended to poke a hole in the thesis.

'In this case it isn't. What we are dealing with here is a clash of cultures. And culture is man made. It's not genetic.'

'That is precisely my point...'

Marloff picked up the photograph to wave it in the air.

'Just look at it,' he said. 'A culture clash if ever I saw one. Look at them. Teutonic, romantic Annette, and pragmatic, prehensile Giusi. We have to deal with them as they are. Forget that neo-Darwinism lurking in that Puritan skull of yours squealing to get out. We have to deal with these people as they are. Base our judgements on objective analysis. Mario has no sense of wrongdoing. And neither has the girl Giusi. Life for them is a business. A sequence of deals and bargains where things have to be worked to the best advantage. Particularly their own. Conscience doesn't come in to it. In any case they haven't killed anyone.'

'Not yet.'

Griffiths gave his interim verdict in such a gloomy voice. Marloff burst out laughing. He reached out to shake his friend's arm in a gesture of unstinting friendship. They had been friends and colleagues and collaborators for a long time. Griffiths began to chuckle himself.

'Come on then,' he said. 'Out with it Anton Marloff. Speculation is sparks and smoke. Knowledge is power. Especially when you deal with "people like these". I quote you.'

He extracted a fresh cigar from a packet and waved it to evoke a symphony of information before wedging it in his loose, melancholy mouth. Marloff was a linguist and his command of Italian dialects was a source of continuing admiration and envy. Griffiths had the more ample financial resources. They made him all the more intent on equipping himself with as deep a knowledge as possible of the customs and practices and folk ways of the place they were likely to settle. Here Marloff was the expert and he was the only one versed in the saga of Annette Vennenberg.

'You remember Vennenberg?'

'Vaguely. Of course I do.'

'Well now this young thing was his missus.'

'Mistress?'

'Okay. Mistress first. Then missus.'

Marloff tapped the fair girl's image with a fingernail. Griffiths leaned forward to study the three seated so close together at the end of a table.

'Looks more like a tomb than a trattoria,' he said. 'Those red eyes belong to the inferior regions. Where's Vennenberg anyway? I don't see his ghost.'

'Well there she is,' Marloff said. 'The fair Annette. You could say our future is in her hands. Or their hands.'

Griffiths pulled a face to demonstrate distaste and disapproval.

'It's only a transaction,' he said. 'If it comes to that. That's negotiation, not fate.'

'How did she come by her wealth? After all property is wealth. That's fate if you ask me.'

'You amaze me.'

'Do I. In what way? Do tell me.'

'You've no religion and acres of supersition. That's one thing. And then this curiosity about people. Detached and yet insatiable. I mean this girl for example. "What's Hecuba to him or he to Hecuba...?" What's Annette to you or you to Annette? Eh?'

'Peasant origins. Limited horizons. That's you, Griffiths, old fruit. I'm only a poor old cousin-in-law trying to bring a little colour and variety into the monotony of your daily life...'

They were happy to tease each other, seated on the terrace on a warm evening, and to reminisce about old misadventures and mistakes that could no longer blight the settled course of their careers. Since they deserted the groves of academe their promotion at Geneva had been slow but reassuringly steady. Now they were in sight of those comfortable pensions. Pooling their resources would give them a wider choice of suitable havens in which to settle.

'I was always a bit sorry for him.'

Marloff assumed a pose of Olympian detachment. This tranquil interlude on the terrace was a fine balance between a satisfactory past and a secure future. Villa Louisa was a favourite holiday haunt to return to. Behind them was the classic facade of a sixteenth-century palazzo converted into an old-fashioned hotel: through the lines of oleander and myrtle below them, steps led to the stone jetties nudged by painted boats.

'Let us not speak ill of the dead. Old Vennenberg was a decent chap. He had his weaknesses of course. But then don't we all.'

Marloff touched his trim white moustache with his knuckle. Griffiths noted the habitual twitch. Marloff had once jokingly admitted it grew there to prevent young women looking straight through him. Even in the soft lights of the terrace garden he was conspicuously better dressed and more aware of his appearance than his friend slumping untidily in his chair, fondling his cigar and waiting to be diverted.

'It doesn't need to be a secret any more. He was scared stiff of his students. And worse than that. They knew it. He was liable to spasms of diarrhoea before delivering a lecture. He would swig a stiff whisky before reaching the lectern.'

'I always preferred seminars,' Griffiths said. 'Get a good discussion going and the time passes more quickly. Anyway you can always read lectures.'

'Where did it all come from? That deep insecurity. My guess was it came from having a more brilliant older brother.'

'All I can remember is a tall, thin Swede with a ginger moustache hanging over his mouth. Hence the hangdog look. Wasn't there some trouble about him exploiting the research of one of his students? There you are. The temptations of a man promoted above his true capacity, concentrating on career moves instead of the hard grind. Marloff, my boy, we are well out of it.'

'Annette was bright enough and extremely pretty. I could see it coming. To be honest I rather fancied her myself. That old goat Wagner used to say that nothing stimulates the appetite for research more than the daily proximity of a fuckable young female.'

'Irresponsible old sod. Amazing he never got caught.'

Marloff chuckled and winked.

'Do I detect a note of envy?'

'Nothing of the sort. As you well know all my life I've made a point of being responsible and reliable.'

'And respectable! And who has ever thanked you for it? Except me, I mean.'

Once again he reached across to shake Griffiths' arm with soothing affection.

'And here's me thanking you again. Reliable as a rock, Ellis Griffiths.'

'What about the girl? It's the girl presumably we shall have to deal with. Not Vennenberg's ghost.'

'Ah.'

Marloff raised two fingers to show that they were crossed.

'The fact is, old boy, Vennenberg left his wife and two grown sons for the fair Annette.'

Griffiths shook his head as if he had been given something to think deeply about. They were both silent as they contemplated the ramifications of an old male abandoning the family nest for a younger female. Griffiths sighed.

'It happens so often,' he said.

He was not only regretting the absence of restraint among privileged academics. There were wider implications. Surely every civilisation depended in the end on some form or other of systematic restraint? It disturbed him that even at this mature stage in his life there were deep and urgent questions to which he was unable to find a simple answer. Accumulating evidence was always more than an interim activity.

'What was her background? This Annette.'

'She was Annette von Ense. I don't know where the "von" came from.'

Gossip was more relaxing than the effort of distilling precepts. They could enjoy an interlude of unbuttoned frankness. Their wives were safely in bed.

'A solid Augsburg family. Only too solid. The money came from automobile spare parts. Vital I suppose to the German war effort and so on. Anyhow war guilt was the principal agent of family disintegration. You can just imagine it, can't you? Brought up with loving care and bourgeois comfort, Annette becomes an ardent young feminist and in no time at all takes it upon herself to discover the awful truth and she accuses her grandparents and her parents of criminal complicity with Das Dritter Reich. "And as for you," she points across the dinner table at her father whose heart is in poor condition, "You served in the criminal army". She even points her finger at her grosspapa. "How many secrets have you got on your sleeping conscience?" '

'How do you know all this?'

Griffiths spoke quietly to encourage Marloff to keep his voice down.

'Vennenberg told me,' he said.

Griffiths raised an eyebrow to indicate he had no idea Marloff had known Vennenberg so well.

'The appalling honesty of the young,' Marloff said. 'Makes one quite relieved to be childless.'

They both looked more closely at the photograph as though they were seeing Annette for the first time.

'And so her Odyssey began. As far north as Stockholm and as far south as Naples with a spell in Salzburg thrown in. But always those cheques from home never failed to catch up with her. A privileged vagabond. A perpetual student in search of life, liberty and the pursuit of happiness and as much truth as a pampered stomach could stomach. In the end she signed up for Vennenberg's new glamorous course in computerised archaeology and, as the phrase goes, the rest is history.'

'What did she see in him do you think?'

Griffiths seemed anxious to know. It couldn't be put down to nothing more than natural selection and perpetuating the species. It was something between a whim and an illusion and yet it was a vital element in human existence that had to be taken into account.

'What does anybody see in anybody? Maybe she wanted

a more acceptable father? A large nordic figure, soft inside, anxious to please, yearning to be mothered. That's how it goes, Griff. Emotional supply and demand. We can ponder too long over these little things. He was a bit like a large dog, eager to be petted. And she was keen on dogs. And of course there was that distemper of late middle age. The longing to remain youthful.'

Griffiths palpated his expanding stomach with the tips of his fingers.

'I used to worry about that sort of thing,' he said. 'I haven't for ages.'

Marloff still played tennis. Griffiths in no way held this against him. He was content with his own untidiness. He liked to assume it gave him more time to devote to his researches into the nature of truth.

'The twists and turns,' Marloff said. 'There really is no end to it. Quite unexpectedly Vennenberg came into a heap of money.'

'Before or after?'

Griffiths insisted on the proper order of events. Quite apart from establishing hard fact, any gratuitous acquisition of wealth threatened to transform a homily into a fairy tale. Homilies were much more to his taste.

'That I don't know.'

Somehow the small gap in his knowledge only added to the extent of Marloff's omniscience.

'What I do know is that Vennenberg had a brother who was a brilliant biochemist. They didn't get on and didn't have much to do with each other. But the brother died of pancreatic cancer and all the patents and royalties and so forth fell into Vennenberg's lap. To cut a long story short he promptly resigned and came down here and bought these properties that included the ruined castle of Capestri, and he and his beloved Annette set about restoring it together.'

'Would you call it a castle? More like an overblown farmhouse.'

'Marked on the old maps as Castello. He showed it to me. It must have been the year you and Myfanwy didn't come down here. He found books about it. And manuscripts. In some old episcopal library. Excited as a schoolboy. Resolved to write a history of the whole estate. He became absorbed in the enterprise. Medieval archaeology all around him. And an intriguing strata of local superstition. It was haunted. There was a ghost! That's how they got it cheap. A charming ruin in an isolated position with a spectacular view and a romantic couple with pots of money to put into its restoration. They both loved it.'

'Wouldn't suit us though, would it?'

'No. But we've got to admire it. It will help things along.'

'What ghost anyway?'

He was sceptical but still interested. As Myfanwy said when you find a place you've got to know about it. Settle in like good neighbours. 'We don't want to degenerate do we into ex-pats hanging about just for the sun and the booze,' she said. Griffiths had great respect for his wife's good taste.

'An unfaithful Orsini wife tossed over the cliff returns to haunt the place.'

'Hum. We make our own ghosts. Anway, I want somewhere where I can relapse completely into the condition of growing older. Where things won't go bump in the night.'

'Wait till you see it,' Marloff said. 'The photographs don't do it justice. No view of the track through the vineyard. There's work to be done of course. There always is. I think the girls will be very excited by it. Your glass is empty, Griff. Shall we have another? This place isn't too bad, is it?'

Marloff was keen to initiate their habitual competition in generous entertainment. It was one way that had developed over the years through which they could express some regard for each other. Griff lit another of his small cigars on the pretext it would help to keep the gnats away. There were other guests still out on the terrace, some moving with unselfconscious grace between the shadows and the lamplight. The houseboy in his white jacket brought them more brandy, shuffling his shoes in the gravel.

'A few years back I dropped in there on my way to Rome and there she was, the fair Annette, on top of a ladder plastering a hole in the dining room wall. High up it was. I was quite alarmed for her. But she was laughing like a schoolgirl on holiday. Working as hard as her grandfather ever did with his automobile spare parts. She had never been so happy. She said so. Such energy. With these German genes hard labour conquers all, including an inclination to slide into depressions. Vennenberg was so proud of her. You could say she gave him new life. He was borrowing her youth. Smiling and smirking at her he was, all through lunch. I felt quite an intruder. They were totally absorbed in the house and the garden. And each other.'

'A Garden of Eden just made for two... and now enter the snake.'

With lugubrious humour Griffiths waved his cigar over the image of Mario in the photograph.

'Not at all. At least not in the way you seem to anticipate, Pastor Griffiths. Vennenberg never knew Master Mario. Or if he did, only as a peripheral relative of the egregious Salvatore.'

'A different snake?'

'Nothing of the kind. An employee. A general factotum and fount of local wisdom. Vennenberg used to repeat Salvatore's comical pronouncements. You could call him a cunning clown, but he wasn't a snake.'

Griffiths' face clouded with suspicion. He wanted to know more about Marloff's sources of information.

'I saw a lot of Vennenberg that year. He was a very good host when he could take his eyes off Annette.'

'So you stayed there?'

'Once or twice. Very cultivated chap, Vennenberg. Laid down an excellent cellar. And he took a real interest in dialects as well as medieval history. Very good on Belli.'

'Who's Belli?'

'Roman dialect poet. Vennenberg wanted to turn Capestri into a late medieval version of the Garden of the Hesperides with lemons instead of golden apples. The vineyard of course and the almond orchard. And the dogs. A breed of white shepherd dogs from the Maremma.'

'So where's the bloody snake?'

Griffiths was irritated by his own ignorance. If there were snags in the enterprise ahead he wanted to be made fully aware of them. Myfanwy and Marjorie were enthusiastic gardeners and liable to be dazzled by vivid evocations of the fecundity of the Capestri district. There was too much un-diluted pseudo-medieval romanticism being allowed to pass unchecked.

'Well there you are.'

Marloff took his time to relish Griffiths' undivided attention. At least as long as the pause lasted the wealth of information equalled the capital resources Griffiths controlled.

'Not a character you see. Not a person. The cruel blow came from Providence disguised as our old friend Impartial Nature. Without that they could have gone on enjoying the fruits of the earthly paradise for many a long year. Vennenberg, poor chap, was struck down by the very enemy within that destroyed his brother. So that you could say, if you were looking at it with cold scientific objectivity, the very cell that brought him great wealth also sealed his fate.'

Griffiths resisted the temptation to dispute Marloff's use of the word Providence. It was a concept that had worried him since childhood. The zeal of his ancestors had evaporated under the pressure of time and tolerance, but he remained uneasy in the role of detached observer. There had to be more to life than seeking out the most comfortable niche and settling in it.

'The fact is Vennenberg saw it coming, and he was terrified.'

They paid a brief homage of silence as they contemplated the awesome power of disease.

'How old was he? When he knew.'

'Rolf Vennenberg, middle fifties. The girl Annette, early thirties.'

The facts were cold comfort, like the dates on a tombstone.

'How many years of bliss?'

'That I can't tell you. Ten maybe. Maybe less. Who can measure bliss?'

'There you are.'

Griffiths derived some satisfaction from the admission.

'The devil is always in the detail.'

'All I can say is, I saw it. And it existed. And then I suppose it was washed away in a tidal wave of anxiety. The search was on for the miracle cure. What else was all that money good for? Clinics and sanatoria all over the place. Paris, Berlin, Stockholm, and God knows where else. She never left his side, all devotion and dedication, so that obsequious creature Salvatore was left in complete charge at Capestri. He had the run of the place, not to mention the use of Annette's Fiat. His family were in and out. The Vennenbergs came back and forth of course, and there were the friends of a kind they had dotted here and there, within calling distance. Mostly Germans, Swedes and Swiss as it happens. And there was that so-called Principessa, Elena Cristina, who declared herself devoted to Annette, and specialised in knowing everything about everybody. Salvatore was a bit scared of her. But if he bobbed and bowed and scraped enough he usually got away with it. In any case it was generally assumed that Salvatore the loyal retainer was worthy of all his perks. The amazing thing is the wealth kept on coming. Annette's grandfather and then her father died, and in rolled another fortune.'

'But it didn't do away with the problem. Vennenberg's fears.'

'She drowned them,' Marloff said. 'Cures and alcohol ran together. First she poured out for him and then he insisted she join him. Bliss dissolved into an alcoholic haze. And so it went on to the end. His end I mean.'

'Humm.'

Griffiths could only grunt the misgiving he had that death could ever be that easy.

'He wanted to be cremated but that proved to be too difficult, which is odd, considering all the money they had. Maybe she was too drunk to organise the trip to Perugia. To make up for the mess, she had him buried in an imitation Orsini tomb in the garden. This was useful. Annette transferred her dedication and devotion to the garden, the house, and the dogs. In that order. She told the Principessa she would live alone there to the end of her days. She had enormous faith in the dogs. She believed they could still see him around. Or at least his ghost.'

Griffiths gave a sigh and took a consoling sip of brandy.

'What a species,' he said. 'Dogs know more than we do.'

'Come on Griff. Cheer up. I thought you had come to the conclusion that there was some form of salvation lurking on the edge of the universe.'

Marloff made a brief sequence of gestures in the balmy night air to indicate an all-embracing and comforting view of the human condition. Griffiths muttered phrases about lost sheep having no health in them.

'I wouldn't call the fair Annette a lost sheep,' Marloff said. 'All that worldly wealth. Don't we call it worldly because it gives us worlds to command?'

'Money doesn't buy youth, Marloff. Or wisdom. In the end we are all victims.'

'Oh dear. Just listen to him. Sweet melancholy. Only those with a good bank account can afford to indulge in it. The Salvatores of this world spend all their energies on avoiding becoming victims. Imagine it. He saw his chance. A wealthy young widow locking herself up a lonely tower. There he was a pagan countryman tying up his vines and watching a young woman, as he might have put it, denying the forces of nature. There was a need to be gratified and there had to be something in it for all the family. Don't look so disapproving. It's the way they've looked at things from time immemorial. All he had to do, as you might say, was to find the right opening for his vigorous young cousin Mario, just finishing his military service. Who better to help in the garden! Imagine the hints and whispers in Salvatore's cantina. "Listen. You come and work for me. I can't pay you much as you know. But this young widow... she's lonely. I need some help in the garden. The roof needs attention and I can't climb like I used to. And you know about cars and that old car of hers... she likes it. You make it go better." '

'And so the serpent crawled into the garden after all.'

Griffiths picked up the photograph to look at the bare muscular arms of the young man in the middle and the terracotta flask in front of him.

'Not so much crawled,' Marloff said. 'Jumped! One day while she stood at the window he tumbled off the roof and landed in some bushes. He jumped to his feet laughing and his arms stretched forward like a footballer who had just scored a goal.'

'She fell in love with him?'

'According to the Principessa she did. Principessa tried to put up a warning hand but that put a stop to her visits. There were no limits to Mario's priapic powers. People could only get at her through him.'

'What about this other one?'

Griffiths tapped the figure on Mario's left in the photograph.

'He looks quite happy here sandwiched between the two.'

'Yes. Well that's Giusi. During his military service in Calabria, Master Mario had become engaged to Maria Giuseppina Vizzini. That's little Giusi. Then the warrior

123

returned home and working, so to speak, so hard at Capestri, he conveniently forgot Maria Giuseppina. Slipped his mind. Until Giusi's babbo turned up all gold rings and bracelets. You could say dressed to kill.'

'Oh dear,' Griffiths said. 'This sounds like opera without music. You are about to tell me the mighty Mario had to plead for his life.'

'In a sense yes. But to Annette, not to Vizzini. There were startling reports of a meeting in Salvatore's cantina. Not in the house, according to the Principessa, out of respect for Vennenberg's ghost. Mario stuck out his chest and demanded marriage and an immediate flight to Germany. It wasn't a case of him being afraid of Vizzini but there was an entire clan to contend with. In any case Annette had all the money in the world to finance any kind of transfer. And he, Mario, would quite like to see the world in comfort. She would have none of it. She was married to Capestri and to Vennenberg's ghost. How could she possibly marry a peasant who couldn't tell the difference between German and English? He had obliged her and served her well but he was no more worthy of marriage to an educated heiress than one of her dogs. It got very heated. In the end Mario stalked out to meet his Calabrian obligation. He had been so hurt, so wounded, he would never return to Capestri. Never!'

'Well he did,' Griffiths said. 'He must have done. And there's this photograph to prove it.'

'People are strange.'

A liturgical note crept into Marloff's voice. He spoke so

softly that Griffiths had to lean forward like a man sharing a secret.

'Up there it seemed that Vennenberg would be canonised. He had come from nowhere like wandering saints used to do and his wealth had brought a new prosperity to the district. Village children brought flowers to lay on his tomb. Annette took to wearing his old jackets and began to look like the high priestess of the cult. The dogs were a problem. They bit her arms and legs but she didn't feel it. Anaesthetised by alchohol. Then Salvatore's old aunt was bitten. She died in fact of natural causes but Annette paid out some compensation. Mario turned up for the funeral. Annette's car wouldn't start. Mario fixed it.'

'Aha.'

'Aha nothing. Everything is an accident until it happens. Then it becomes Fate. Mind you Salvatore was always on the look out to give Fate a helping hand. He could see through the window a woman peering in the mirror to search out the wrinkles around her eyes.'

'Just the facts,' Griffiths said. 'Never mind the fancy bits.'

'Salvatore sent messages south. It was time for Mario and Giusi to move back. There was a convenient apartment vacant at Ponte Gavello no more than seven kilometres away. Then Mario was back in the garden so that Annette could see the sweat rolling off his bare back. It became part of her routine to watch Giusi bring the mighty Mario his food and flask of wine. The turning point came when Giusi ran into the old servant's hall screaming and begging Annette to stop

125

Mario going windsurfing. She had had a dream of losing him in a sudden storm, and the women of her clan had a second sight which was as much a curse as a gift...'

'Southern superstition versus northern romantic illusion,' Griffiths said.

'Well there was a storm. Mario didn't go. And there was a man drowned. From that time on Annette treated Giusi with a new respect. She was in the house as much as Mario was in the garden. When Giusi became pregnant, Annette stopped being jealous. They came to an arrangement.'

'That's what it all amounts to in the end,' Griffiths said. 'Living arrangements.'

'Every Sunday Giusi and Mario take over the kitchen and make Annette a splendid meal. They keep on filling her glass until she's in a satisfactory stupor and then they put her to bed. You can see from the photograph Annette is a pretty hopeless drunk. The Principessa says she is worn down by wealth and committing suicide by stealth. She thinks Mario is after the place.'

Griffiths struggled to his feet to stretch himself.

'God! What a world,' he said.

'There are murmurs of disapproval in the village.'

'What's it got to do with me? I'm just a narrow-minded old maid anyway...'

'Mario's the man to deal with.'

Marloff was absorbed in his own penetrating assessment of the situation. He held out both hands to indicate that in the final analysis a comfortable place in the world was like a balance sheet where profit and loss were the essential factors.

'In this harsh world, Griff, if you want to get anywhere, you sometimes have to do business with the devil. It's a marvellous cascina. Great potential. It can only go up in value. Marjorie will love it. And Myfanwy of course. That goes without saying.'

'I'm not sure we'd fit in up there. Settle I mean. Planted. For good, for heaven's sake.'

Marloff hastened to reassure him.

'Detachment, Griff old dear. Cultivate observation. "Italy! Paradise of exiles." There's a lot to be said for polite indifference. Minding your own business. Don't idealise anywhere. Immoderate love turns so easily to immoderate hate. It's only a photograph. You can see the two women have come to an understanding. Who knows one day if he misbehaves they'll turn on him! Life in the sweet south, Griff, old boy. Let's have another beakerful.'

Griffiths shook his head.

'I don't know. If I have to stay here I want a bedroom with a window facing north.'

'And a curlew calling?'

Marloff laughed, gripped his arm and drew him along the terrace for a last look at the lake in the moonlight. In the distance someone afloat was singing to the strains of a guitar.

'Let's sleep on it,' Marloff said. 'Wrap yourself in moonlight and luscious music. This is the place to be!'

Nomen

WHEN the wars were over and the skies began to clear he appeared among us as if he had always been there. He could have been another casualty since he appeared even stiffer than we were in the open air, yet we accepted him for the most part as a good omen. He was so ready to appear as one of us: the same waxen pallor, the same rodent brightness in the wide-open eyes. A more flexible mouth perhaps capable of greater extremes of joy and sadness. In any case his voice was melodious and we were very ready to listen to anything he might have to say.

The young in danger and sharing the same stressful circumstances easily congeal and coagulate and for those first few days of blissful ceasefire we stuck together. Without being oratorical or loquacious, in that low vibrant voice that so easily commanded our attention, he said how lucky we were to have survived in such good condition and the implication was the world was still there for us to repossess. Even transformations were possible. He emphasised the word new, as if it had never been used before, in several languages; until he settled on the dialect that he understood

131

was native to us. We called him Nomen, and he didn't object. He was with us to reassure us. It was a new dawn and so it could be a new beginning. The girl called Candida was a little older than most of us, a postgraduate she said, and therefore harder to satisfy.

'All dawns are new,' she said. 'All they do is announce the here and now. What we have to decide is what we are going to do about it. What country, for example, what constitution, what style, and what century even if, as you say, the choice is ours. For my part, I have to tell you, I see the world and all its pathetic histories from a proactive woman's point of view.'

It was clear she was struggling to resist his sympathetic smile. We were able to move freely out of our dark corner of the deserted city because he knew his way through the open sewers and the shattered streets. In the chaos of war you can acquire an affection for ruins. They offer a minimum of shelter, and bombs in their own way are a form of excavation. They give a glimpse of the strata of the centuries. It all seems so old it makes you feel invincibly young. In what had been the palace gardens, headless statues leant at awkward angles among the blasted trees and he had some difficulty in persuading us to follow him to the tranquil lakes where he assured us we would begin to feel things differently.

'There are fish in the lake still,' he said. 'And Pepe Pescatore knows just how to catch them and grill them.'

For so long it seemed trucks had rattled through the empty streets carting away corpses. Now as if by magic he found an empty truck and we climbed into it, a living cargo, and he drove us away singing half-remembered songs like children on an outing. Could it be a return to innocence on which to build a regenerated world? By the lake, he assured us, we could rest and recuperate and decide what course to take. When we ran out of tunes I could hear Candida muttering to herself as she clung to the rail above the driving cab.

'Do we have any choice?' she was saying. 'We've lived on Illusions for so long. They kept us going. Now we are being rolled out on the road to Reality. Can we stand it? They say the Tyrant is dead. But in my mind he was dead and buried long ago under a great mound of wishful thinking.'

I was far more inclined to sing. The death of the Tyrant and the end of the war were surely facts to sing about. When the guns are silent you can hear the birds singing. He drove our truck through the trees and the walls of reeds and rushes to where the fisherman moored his boats in secret at the narrow end of the lake. The evening sun turned the shallow water into gold and through a gap in the reeds we caught our first glimpse of the two islands in the distance and on one of them a bell tower that stood intact. This was Pepe's kingdom, of no strategic value, ignored by the missiles and advancing troops in too much of a hurry to stop and lay the place waste. There were deep wells and caves on both islands where Pepe had hidden barrels of wine and demijohns of olive oil and bags of flour. We were rowed over to Bell Island and next to the ruined church there was a barn of delightful antiquity that Pepe was resolved to convert into a tavern. Nothing had ever tasted so good as the white fish, the rosé wine, and the thick brown bread. Pepe and his old mother took such pleasure in watching us eat we felt like cheerful characters assembled at the happy ending of a fairy story. Along the walls behind us there were white marble Roman tombstones and Candida took obvious pleasure in deciphering the inscriptions while she sipped her wine. She became eloquent and began to insist that the future simply had to be different otherwise the wheel of Fate would just turn and present us with the same old sequence of calamities. She was ready to formulate transforming remedies. The world should be placed under the control of women. The terrors of technology could best be contained by an oligarchy of highly qualified women. Bombing would be banned. Just as the Chinese mandarins had restricted the use of gunpowder, a revered order of lady doctors of philosophy would be in charge of technology and might even transform control panels into shining altars of worship. There was much light-hearted discussion of the merits of the great world religions for future use. Could they at last be empowered to calm mankind's unruly fevers and bring rest to the multitudes as much as to the chosen few? In our unusual state of repletion and contentment the murmur of mild contention was enough to send us into a long untroubled sleep.

When I opened my eyes to meet the morning sunlight and the smiling faces around me, it was as if the years of war had never happened. What was that old hymn about the thousand ages being forgotten as a dream that dies at the opening day? All around me was the embryo of a new society and I saw it reflected in Nomen's smiling face. The days would be so full we would forget to count them. By mid morning the waters of the lake would be warm enough to swim in, and by the evening Pepe would take those who cared to join him night-fishing by the light of the moon. It soon became the custom for Candida to take two or three companions with her to weed and chatter in Pepe's garden and to harvest any produce under his mother's benevolent instruction. There was everything to keep us occupied and no compulsion. Nomen listened sympathetically when I told him this was the first time in my life I had not felt an urgent need to move on. No scratching about for food and shelter. No scramble to hide. He called this a small reason to rejoice. In which case, I wondered, what would be a great reason and how much greater would be the rejoicing? Everything he said was resonant with meaning and I listened as intently as I could and yet struggling to remember let alone memorise. I was too content with the springtime of life around me and perhaps his words combined too well with the language of the lakeside. His voice melted too easily into the music of the moment.

One of our number, Alberto, was particularly eager to organise games. Alongside the lake there was an area of firm level sand that we could use. With some ingenuity he created bats and balls of various sizes and we spent time in the evenings devising rules and regulations without which, as Alberto insisted, there would be no purpose or pattern to the activity. Myself I imagined we hardly needed a purpose. This was an interval of bliss to restore our spirits before turning to the tasks of building a city where healthy children could play unthreatend in the streets and gardens.

That morning one of Alberto's games was in progress when we were astonished to witness three women in torn dresses racing along the margin of the lake pursued by a gang of youths wearing red scarves and brandishing knives and shears. The eldest of the three women was the first to stumble. They caught up with her as she fell into the water and bent her arms behind her back and began to shear off all her hair. They were rough about it. Blood streamed down her face as she screamed for help. As we watched, the younger women were captured and dragged along by their hair to suffer the same punishment. When they became aware of an audience the youths grew more violent. They shouted that these women had consorted with the Tyrant's storm troops. They were treacherous whores and due for retribution.

I heard Nomen muttering to himself. He was pale with an anger I had never seen him show before. He was deploring something he called the awesome versatility of the Devil in words I barely understood. He stood before the gang of young men and demanded they release the women. For a moment it appeared they would accept his authority. Then one of their number shouted he was a collaborator. Even as we watched they turned on the man we had accepted as our leader. In a collective frenzy they stabbed him repeatedly with their knives and shears. His blood soaked in the sand. They stood appalled at what they had done before they fled and left him bleeding to death on the ground. To our lasting shame we never sprang to his defence. We were unarmed, we told ourselves to excuse our cowardice. We were appalled as much by our paralysis and inertia as by the speed of the terrible event. He was bleeding to death as we trembled and then tried to attend to his wounds. Candida and her group did what they could. We were so unprepared. We had seen death and destruction but this was something different. We were more in awe of him as he lay still than when he talked to us. Could he have been so perfect when he was alive? Within hours he was embalmed in our memory. From the moment he lay on the marble altar in the church with a bell tower, we began the painful struggle to recall the things he had said. Were they meant as lessons and prescriptions or were they only sequences of memorable phrases? Candida and her group were loudest in their grief. They called him the man who defended women. It became clear to me as soon as he was buried, the island would become the centre of a cult and Candida would play a central part in its development. For the rest of us there would be little left except to struggle with memories before we faced the world and its recycled burden of incurable infirmities. How much light and guidance could his vanishing voice offer us in what already threatened to be the gathering of a new darkness? Would we ever find again a person so intent on sharing the freshness of the world with the people living in it, every newborn child inheriting the newborn day?

Home

'YOU mustn't keep on going over it,' my son Daniel says. 'It won't bring him back and it won't help you.'

He is quite right of course. But I keep on going over it. Dennis groaning like an animal in pain; turning that awful colour and his eyes sticking out of his head and me pulling desperately at the communication cord. I am gasping for breath myself, the green and purple colours of hell appear whichever way I look. The ambulance on the deserted station platform in the dead of night and the sudden pitiless light in the emergency room at the hospital in Viterbo. A place that Dennis used to love and I never want to see again.

'Look, mama,' Daniel said. 'You are only seventy-three. These days that is nothing. You could have ten even twenty years ahead of you.'

My son Daniel, always good at counting: beats to a bar and rates of interest. By the time he had finished in the Royal College of Music he had become an expert in share dealing. He said it would make up for the insecurity of being a clarinet player in a world stuffed with clarinettists. Well before he was thirty Daniel made a fortune in some aspect of the recording business that his father looked down his nose at.

'The thing is, Dilys Myfanwy, you'll have to learn to stand on your own feet.'

True enough. And the trace of reprimand. As he sees it I lived in his father's pocket and he was incarcerated in a wretched boarding school in Kent while his parents went off in hot pursuit of his father's brilliant career.

'You can go where you like,' my son Daniel says. 'You can do what you like. Think of it as a new adventure.'

I had more than enough adventure with Dennis, more than forty years of it. I was dazzled by his accomplishments. He could speak six languages, take an engine to bits and put it together again, he was an accomplished pianist. He was no matinée idol to look at, but he had a beautiful, seductive voice and a dashing, carefree manner that many women liked, and yet he chose me. He was red haired and impetuous to the point of being explosive, but with me he was a little lamb, always warm, loving, devoted. Whenever he went off on some film safari without me, which was not often – he said I was his right and left hand rolled into one – he always rushed back to me, panting for love and reassurance.

'If you want to settle down, you can settle wherever you like. You've lived in goodness knows how many places: Lucca, Aix en Provence, Klagenfurt, Piansano and goodness knows where else. You must know which will suit you best by now!'

Wherever. That's the trouble. When Dennis was alive I never thought anywhere in Europe was foreign. Wherever we went he was always accepted because he spoke the language so perfectly and had the manners to go with it and the exotic surname of Macphail. Things always went swimmingly until he lost his temper at some blatant piece of chicanery. He was easily taken in, in spite of his brilliance. Without him, everywhere becomes cold and hostile and foreign and I am like the proverbial pilgrim in a foreign land. None of his accomplishments were mine so what am I without him? I can't cling to my son Daniel. That is the last thing he would want.

'You know money is no problem.'

Not any more. Has not been for sometime. Daniel is rich and generous. But I would rather have Dennis back and all his problems. I was useful then. It used to make me laugh, the pride he took in his lack of business sense. 'Money never meant much to the Macphails,' he said. A breed of Anglican clerics, including a bishop and several colonial administrators. Daniel was quick to point out that his father had no religion and a fine contempt for British imperial pretensions. They were so different my husband and my son. What could I do about it? Just find some corner to curl up and die.

In Rome I spoke to that dear old Viennese Herr Doktor Fischer. He was always nice about Dennis, and Dennis was more patient than usual listening to him. 'He knows a lot,' Dennis would say, wagging his head mysteriously as if to suggest the Herr Doktor had access to arcane depth that his own linguistic skills had never penetrated.

'Dear Mrs Macphail,' he said. 'Think of the world as you knew it before you ever met Dennis.'

I shook myself to make the effort. Somewhere in the mists of the mid-twentieth century I was considered a bright girl who had clambered out of a Welsh nonconformist background via academia to the sunlit uplands of the London BBC. I must have believed something like that myself. A clever little girl delighting in her own cleverness. My mother was proud of me, but not so proud perhaps as she was of my brother Silin who became a distinguished physician and took up a professorial chair in Sydney, Australia. Poor thing, she never saw him again. Family pride moves in mysterious ways. I am still ashamed of the sacrifices my parents made on their miserable ministerial wages (never more than three hundred pounds per annum) to secure educational advantage for their two children.

'Think back through your life, dear Mrs Macphail. Where were you happiest?'

The answer was one I had used before, particularly when I was most exasperated with Dennis, but I never thought of it as a compass point to where I might settle. Gelliwen. My grandfather's modest smallholding. All of thirty-eight acres. I knew the name of every field and paddock. It was wartime but that meant nothing to a child of five or six. The whole world of the island was under intense cultivation then. There was happiness there, unalloyed, like riding home from Cae Pella, the furthest field, on the back of what felt like a huge cart horse. (I can still smell the leather collar they called mwnci and feel the gentle sway of the unhurried progress, my fingers clutching the coarse hair of Capten's mane.)

'Daniel, I think I know exactly where I'd like to try to settle.'

'If settle you must.'

He gives me a smile that suggests after all he likes me in his tolerant way.

'Gelliwen.'

He frowns with an effort to recall although he surely must have heard the name before. Or had he? Yet another little stab of guilt. There were so many gaps in communication in years gone by that could never be filled.

'Sir Fôn,' I said. 'That's what we called it in those days. Never Ynys Môn or Anglesey.'

In his reserved way he showed approval. It was of course the backwoods as far as his world was concerned, but within easy reach. Near enough for him to visit me at will and far enough to keep me outside the sphere of his activities.

★★★

It was disconcerting to descend on Sir Fôn on the magic carpet of Daniel's millions. I don't know whether he realises how much the power of his wealth impresses me. I hope he doesn't. I struggle to maintain a sense of proportion. This place both is and is not Sir Fôn as I knew it. There are things that can't be changed, the contours of a geology that my poor father was so ridiculously proud of: from the top of

Penmynydd, Mynydd Caergybi, Mynydd Mechell and Mynydd Bodafon stick out of the horizon as they have always stuck out; and looking south, from the Gogarth to Yr Eifl the noble range of Eryri has not changed: how could it? Beaches can't change much, nor the untidy tilt of the rocks as they pile on top of each other.

I must begin with Gelliwen. Find a still centre in my confused world. Daniel is being patient with me. On the farm lane, which is rough and stonier than I remember, he allows me to take his arm. He listens to my reminiscence. I point to a boulder. It was there, according to my grandfather, that his Uncle Owain hid his carpenter's tools before emigrating to America without saying goodbye to his mother. The farm was too small to keep them all. But they wrote to each other for the rest of their lives. My father deposited the letters in the County Archives along with his notebooks and the other bits and pieces he found so interesting. I linger over the little spring that never ran dry. My grandfather would not drink any other water. It is choked now with wild watercress, but still there.

The house was a horrid ruin. The roof leaking and the windows boarded with rusty corrugated zinc iron. The out-houses collapsing, open to the elements, offering shelter to cattle. The great oak tree, in what was the paddock, stands as monument to walls and hedgerows that have disappeared forever.

'This is where my father was born. Gelliwen.'

I had cherished a hope Daniel could have taken a picture

of me on the path to the front door where thyme and rosemary grew on either side. There was nothing there except mud trampled by the cattle and, where the door had been, more rusty corrugated zinc iron.

'He loved the place. We all did. From our bleak manse in the quarrying village it seemed the earthly paradise across the straits. And look at it now.'

'I don't really remember him,' Daniel says. 'I was in that school in Sevenoaks when he died. Before that I hardly ever saw him.'

I am pierced with guilt. I put my poor widowed father, the Reverend John Roberts, BA, BD, in a Ministers' Retiring Home in a part of the country he never liked so that I could accompany Dennis on his brilliant erratic career to nowhere in the end. There is still no centre. People are in permanent orbit like the planets. What am I doing here?

Back at the hotel we buy local papers to show what properties there are for sale. There will always be a residue of resentment that I can do nothing to remove. I can't make it up to him. The best I can do is to be grateful and uncomplaining and not be a burden. I can't turn back now. There simply is nowhere to turn back to. He thrives on complete freedom of action. I owe it to him to accept his bounty and find a dwelling where he can visit and I can call home. There is an estate agent and valuation firm called Roberts, Luke and Evans, offering a wide range and it occurs to me that the Roberts could well be a second cousin who became an auctioneer. He would be about my age and auctioneers go on forever or at least their names do. Daniel is not curious.

'Better not to do business with relatives,' he says quite firmly.

I can see that. He prefers to use his wealth and the screen of his surname. In any case homosexuals avoid family entanglements. At least he did.

We were filming at an archaeological site in Anatolia, the kind of work that Dennis loved, when Daniel's wife Heather telephoned on a bad landline. She sounded hysterical which was not like her. A still calm is part of her dark beauty. Daniel had left her, and had gone to live with a Swedish millionaire called Axel. They had a place on a Greek island. Dennis was furious and disgusted. Couldn't bear to believe his only son had turned out to be a queer. Dennis had a thing about queers in the business forming cabals to promote each other. He believed a bunch of them had done his early career a lot of harm. The poor old darling never realised it could have been his own impetuous and explosive nature that might have done him damage.

He took the high moral ground. 'What about Marian and Gabriel?' he said. 'My God, how self-absorbed can you get?' As it turned out Heather and the children were well taken care of. They lived in a beautiful house outside Marlow. Marian was the resilient one. I worried about Gabriel. He was highly intelligent and beautiful like his mother and just as shy and sensitive. Heather was a gifted harpist. She had a career of her own, but she preferred teaching. Dennis began to take an interest in his grandchildren, of whom to be honest, up to that point he had been barely, though benevolently, aware. The trouble was there was little we could do to help them. Our commissions were drying up. Dennis decided he would retire. 'I'm sixty-seven next birthday,' he said. 'Time to cash in the chips and enjoy ourselves.' That was all very well except there were precious few chips to cash in. I was seven years younger and I could have worked but he needed me more than ever. What would a renewed, youthful irresponsibility be worth without me as a partner in crime? All we needed to do now was enjoy ourselves. We spent a dozen years looking at megaliths all over the place and embarked on such amateurish enterprises as a photographic record of remote churches in southern Italy.

Dennis never chose to be aware that it was his son that was making all this possible. Our current account was never empty and he never enquired too closely why this should be so. 'I don't know a thing about money,' he would say. 'Dilys looks after the cheque books. These Euros are jolly handy things. Marvellous idea.' Because we moved about so much everybody was glad to see him. I think I've moved about too much.

'Daniel, my son, you are wonderful,' I say. 'I trust your judgement. I think you understand me better than I do myself!'

***

So, here I am. Mrs Macphail, Henefail. The lady of a minia-ture manor. 'A quite delightful conversion and extension of the old smithy, surrounded by trees on the north side, a flourishing garden and a garage space for at least two cars.'

'I only need one,' I murmured. 'And a small one at that.' Nobody heard me. The thrusting young estate agent has been quite cowed by my son Daniel's prolonged silences and aura of affluence. What it is to have a son who is a multi-millionaire ex-clarinettist! Ah, the seductive power of wealth. My father resisted it as a temptation. My husband resented it as an impediment to freedom. My son revels in it. I never witnessed Daniel in action before. So cold and formidable, so unlike his amiable if explosive father and pliable mother. There was a choice of properties and we visited them all in three days.

'Take your time,' he said. 'Bear in mind what you most want to do once you're here.'

He was restrained and patient with me but I made an effort to speed up the process. It did occur to me that his intense concern for my welfare was some form of restitution for having disappointed his father. Or was I transposing my own resolve to sort my father's papers, put them in order and even publish them, with the County Archives permission, something he always intended to do, something I could have helped him with, instead of gallivanting around the world with my beloved, dashing Dennis? I had some expertise in editing. Peter Fry offered me a job in the Documentary Script Unit. That was before Dennis. A nice man Peter. I remember he was much taken with me, but not his face or even his voice. No more than a face in a crowd. When fateful choices we make, etcetera.

Anyway here I am. Lady of the manor complete with faithful retainers. A part-time gardener and a daily help. It is a warm late September and I can still sit in the garden so long as I don't get in Wil Hafan's way. There is a lot to do. The garden has been neglected most of the summer and Wil Hafan regards it all with his own brand of cheerful disapproval. The hedges are overgrown and he particularly dislikes a great clump of pampas grass that is quite out of control, its leaves sticking out like thin knives in all directions. Spiders' webs glitter from one overgrown plant to the other and it comforts me to stare at them as though they meant something more than a decoration, which of course they do. Daniel when he was a little boy told me a fly would need to be five hundred times stronger in order to break out of the web. Or was it six hundred? I might dare to ask him next time he calls. Or I might not. A family is a web too. I turn my attention to a single bramble branch, which stretches down from the tip of a cypress hedge to the broad leaves of a peony as if it were looking for something to hold onto. It dangles like a red rope, with clusters of young green leaves every foot or so on the way down. Wil Hafan with his spade and billhook is moving systematically closer along the border and I wonder how long the briar will be spared. I see more of the seat of Wil's thick trousers than his face. He is older than I am, but determined to go on working. He says he can understand people wanting to live in Sir Fôn, but is mystified by anyone wanting to leave it. He tells me he was born in a village called Paradwys, Paradise, so why on earth should he want to live anywhere else? He is very partial to gnomic utterance and no doubt encouraged by the way I listen to him. Sooner or later I have to ask him if he remembers my grandfather, Evan Roberts, Gelliwen.

The daily help brings him tea and biscuits and I retire indoors. They get on well together, the local man and the Bulgarian refugee. That is what Katica amounts too in the spirit. She still sighs for the roses of Stara Zagora, but she made the mistake of marrying a long-distance lorry driver from Liverpool. He turned out to be violent, and having beaten her up disappeared into Eastern Europe never to be seen again. Katica now lives for the wellbeing of her two children. Rosita is ten and gets bullied at primary school, not because she's foreign, but because she's fat. Her son, Cyril, is fifteen and studious and his mother's pride and joy. Katica was pretty once and struggles to be cheerful but a martyred look can easily pass over her face. Her moods are reflected in her movements. When her spirits are down she tends to slump and drift and sigh. Cleaning becomes an effort.

Both my retainers are anxious to please. Over a few weeks it has become clear to them that I exercise my seigniorial authority through gentle persuasion. A pattern establishes itself. My favourite William Scott hangs on the living-room wall; my Chinese cabinet is in the study along with Daniel's stamp collection and his chess set. With commendable speed everything is in place and everyone knows his or her place. I take a benevolent interest in Wil Hafan's health, which is his chief interest, and in Katica's children. In turn they cherish their routines and accept that I can be absent minded at times because I am engaged in an unspecified literary work worthy of their quiet respect.

***

A corner shop has opened close to the crossroads, opposite the boarded-up chapel and the empty post office premises. An event of great moment. It is no more than a shack really, a former small-scale garage with a corrugated iron roof, but it is brightly lit inside and crammed with everyday necess-ities. Wil Hafan becomes quite lyrical about it: a dove with an olive branch in its beak, flying above the flood of supermarkets threatening to engulf our little world. That sort of thing. Katica was less approving. I urged her to use the corner shop as much as she can. She protested everything costs two or three pennies more. I said it doesn't matter and that pained look passed over her face, suggesting if cost matters so little I should be thinking of paying her a little more. Nothing in the world would please her more than a trip to Bulgaria, but how could she ever afford the fare?

For some time now Katica has had the key to my solid back door so that she can let herself in and I can cultivate the habit of lying in bed late if I feel like it. She can bring me breakfast, which is no more than muesli and goat's yoghurt. She makes fresh coffee the way I like it and she seems to relish the role of a caring and close retainer. This morning she brings me my coffee looking extremely pleased with herself. It seems that Mrs Price the corner shop is a very good person after all. She has a son, Cledwyn, who is in the same form as Katica's son, Cyril. They have become firm friends in the sudden cohesive way that adolescents are capable of. Cledwyn is large and lumbering and Cyril is small, wiry and quick moving. In Katica's view this means they complement each other. She is delighted that they play chess together and go bird-watching and have no taste for football.

I find all this encouraging too. If this is to be my home my father's papers already make me realise a home can't flourish without a neighbourhood. Judging from his sermons, which I admit I find hard going, he seems particularly keen on parables like the good Samaritan that posed the question, 'Who is my neighbour?'

The task I have set myself is daunting. There is an odd chronology driven by my father's family pride. He revels in any resemblance he can detect in the behaviour or appearance between generations, convinced of his own likeness to his great-grandfather and so on. He believed there is a thread that runs through their reaction to events at home or in the world at large, in Wales or in the Middle West, an adherence to principles that continues from the eighteen sixties to the nineteen sixties! No wonder my own youthful response was quiet rebellion and an urge to escape. And yet there is something quite moving in that long correspondence to and fro, from the new world to the old, in the same sober biblical Welsh interspersed with bursts of homely dialect humour. So much to puzzle out. And how to reconcile historical fact with my private myth of a golden age in Gelliwen? There must be some kind of a link between the language of my childhood and the healing process of happiness.

I am meditating these matters when the telephone rings. It is Heather my daughter-in-law. In a cautious sort of way we have always got on. There could have been a touch of envy once. I had a devoted husband. Now we are equal. We can even share a sisterly duty towards each other.

'Dilys.'

That is a good start. It feels supportive.

'Gabriel wants to come to visit you.'

That sounds more of a challenge. From the moment he went to university Gabriel took up extreme positions. Never satisfied until he had been beaten up or spent a night or two in a cell. He never came to Dennis' funeral. Heather said he wasn't fit to be seen. His hair and beard were long and he had taken to sleeping in the back of an ancient Saab, motoring from protest to protest. Heather said he smelt which was an awful pity because he was such a clever, handsome boy. Heather insisted that he wasn't mentally unstable and his attitude had nothing to do with a refusal to take his father's money. When pressed, Heather suggested he suffered from something she called 'world contempt' and it was more than possible he had caught it from herself.

'That's fine,' I say. 'Really. I'd love to see him.'

'He's cleaned up,' she says as though she were reading my thoughts. 'He's very keen to learn about his great-grandfather. Your father that is.'

'Well that's wonderful Heather. That's just what I'm doing myself these days: in a lackadaisical way. If Gabriel came he would sharpen me up. He's such a clever boy. He can stay as long as he likes!'

She moderates my enthusiasm.

'He's not the easiest person to live with. Very outspoken when he feels like it and subject to prolonged silences that can get on your nerves. I know they get on mine.'

I restrain myself from blurting out, 'How like his father'.

'He imagines your father was a protester of some sort. And a bit of a mystic. Is that right?'

'Well, a pacifist anyway,' I say. 'A sort of Welsh Quaker. Poor old boy had to put up with a lot. Anything but a popular preacher.'

Heather couldn't be certain when he would turn up. Gabriel wanted to take a look at Wales first. He knew more about Nicaragua. He wanted to take the temperature, test the water and all that sort of thing. She suggests this would take a week to ten days. In any case he hoped to learn more at the feet of Gamaliel, meaning I suppose my father, and even me.

★★★

I find myself in a state of trembling anticipation. There is a space in my new home for another generation. What a concept to gladden my father's heart. He was so aware of tradition and continuity. If I understand his papers correctly there always needs to be traces of time past in the here and now to make both meaningful. The first thing I will do is take Gabriel to see Gelliwen. This is not just sentiment; or if it is, what better lubricant to a relationship? In my own case it is clear I need something to care about and that means someone to care for, as I did for my dear, dashing Dennis. If the boy is so intrigued by my father's life and way of thinking, who knows what fascinating result could come from such an unusual combination?

It is half term. Cledwyn and Cyril have arrived to give Wil Hafan a hand in removing the overgrown pampas grass. There is a smell of autumn in the air and they are making a bit of a mess trampling the lawn in that corner of the garden. Wil has his little truck attached to the back of his car. He provides the boys with leather hedging gloves to transport those knifelike fronds and he wields a machete to excavate the roots of the massive clump. He will fill the gaping hole and leave a batch of raw soil where he intends to plant fuchsias. He is old and it all takes time and of course I want the place to look attractive when Gabriel arrives; although he was never one to take close notice of his immediate surroundings. Always too wrapped up in his own thoughts I suppose.

To possess my soul in patience as much as anything I take a trip to Mynydd Bodafon. The cloak of mingled ling and heather is very beautiful at this time of the year. And the view from the little summit was always something that set my father's heart swelling with pride. How he used to go on about it and how impatient I was to listen. In the stiff breeze at the top I become aware of the obstacles I shall have to face in dealing with Gabriel; the barriers, language and landscape in their subtle shapes so intimately connected. How much of my father's stuff will I need to translate and how patient will Gabriel be when I try to explain the difficulties? Under this ancient mountain that is really little more than a hill, there still stands the little chapel and field where my grandfather attended an open-air meeting during the religious revival of 1904. A field full of folk in their summer Sunday best, hats wilting in the heat, corsets creaking, the gorse crackling. My father records that the old man experienced a 'heavy sousing' in spite of his dry dissenter spirit. Intriguing to me, but will Gabriel understand that kind of language?

When I return to Henefail I find the boys in the kitchen playing chess. Katica made them all tea, including her daughter Rosita, who I suspect is taking refuge from the threat of bullying by being close to her mother's skirts. Wil Hafan has gone home but the boys are absorbed in their game and Katica is more than happy to watch. They are using my son Daniel's chess set and I am happy that they should do so. It offers a pleasing domestic scene and it has a soothing effect on my nerves.

***

The days are drawing in. Wil Hafan says he is determined to get the garden in apple pie order before Ffair y Borth, that is the old Menai Bridge Hiring Fair. Then he says he will take himself and his missus'cw on a holiday to Bournemouth. 'The ends of the earth,' Wil says. He doesn't care for it but 'his old lady needs pleasing'. There are sounds of altercation in the kitchen. Katica wants Cyril and Cledwyn to take Rosita with them to the fair. They don't want to be lumbered with her. They say there will be a rock concert, with a celebrated Welsh language band playing later on, that Cledwyn wants Cyril to hear. Part of his education, Cledwyn says. Katica says no Rosita, no concert. They have reached an impasse. Just three days left to reach a compromise.

I have heard nothing of Gabriel. Katica and I keep fiddling about in his bedroom, in what we consider attempts to make it more attractive, more homely as she puts it, but I suspect Gabriel doesn't go in for 'homely' much. I have a nice picture of my father framed. He looks bespectacled and ministerial, although he never wore a clerical collar. 'It sets a man apart' he used to say, 'when he should be mixing as an equal among his fellow men.' Although I never saw a man less inclined to mix. You could see him drive himself to be cheerful. I don't know what benefit Gabriel would derive from contemplating his visage and I can't decide whether or not to hang the picture up, and if so, where?

I wonder about this wanting to take a look at Wales first. It sounds suspiciously like those nineteenth, and for that matter twentieth-century guidebooks where the intrepid traveller is advised to advance into the unknown via Chester, Shrewsbury or Gloucester. Was I supposed to answer for the whole country? It was as much as I could do to answer for myself. Especially now that I had no longer to answer for Dennis. I always took the view that everyone should take their nationality for granted and certainly not make a song and dance about it. Under the influence of Dennis, I suppose, I was always inclined to believe that race, religion and nationality were a pain in the neck. Shackles to be broken. He would say the one place he felt most at home was in Lazio, because of the Etruscans not the Italians. The Etruscans were safely dead. The locals very quickly got on his nerves.

Right up to the day of the Fair I was in two minds about phoning Heather. I had no number for Gabriel. I doubted whether he had a mobile. It would be little help to him in his mystical explorations. If I rang Heather it might sound like a weakness. A lonely old woman pining for company and that sort of thing, which is far from the case. What I need is a companion in exploration. There is so much here to find out. We could begin together at the ruin of Gelliwen and fan out from there: to the Middle West of the United States in the nineteenth century and the humbler sphere of the family who stayed at home, and what it all means, if it means anything.

In the end it was Heather who rang me.

'Dilys.'

It sounded as humbly apologetic as Heather could get. I

always felt that inside that shy beauty and musical talent, there was a backbone of steel.

'I'm awfully sorry. Gabriel has gone off to India.'

'Good Lord.'

I try not to sound indignant or disappointed. Quite a balancing act.

'When did that happen?'

'He got as far as Swansea when he met this wonderful Indian girl, Vidya something. They've gone off to an Ashram that she says will provide him with all the answers he is seeking, and her as well of course.'

'But what about all this business of testing the waters in Wales? All that sort of thing.'

I am trying hard not to get personal. She might think I was hurt that he had lost interest in my father and whatever it was he imagined my father stood for. Was Gabriel such an impressionable creature that he could be diverted from his purpose by the first exotic beauty he encountered? And what was he doing in Swansea? Didn't he know that in every country there is always a North and a South? Should I say something about going to Birmingham by way of Beachy Head? I could feel the distance between myself and my daughter-in-law lengthen the longer I waited for a reply.

'He wasn't very impressed quite frankly,' Heather said, 'with what he saw or heard. Second-hand English, he said, obsessed with rugby and being famous and getting their names in lights in the West End. Not very polite really. You know what he's like!'

The sad part was, I didn't. I had been looking forward to opening a door through which he and I could pass together, to reach a new level of understanding. Surely see the things my father cherished were more than dust in a Pharaoh's tomb? Now the door was to remain firmly shut.

'He said it wasn't a place where anything meaningful could happen. Not as things are in the world these days. I'm sorry, Dilys.'

I suppose she was, in her own distant way. Being sorry doesn't mean much without the empathy in sympathy.

★★★

India or Sir Fôn we all belong to the same world in the end. Maybe Gabriel should have come here after all if he wanted to learn something new. Cledwyn and Cyril did go to the Fair. Mrs Price Siop Bach gave Katica reassurances and Rosita was diverted to listening to records with Cledwyn's cousin, Sioned, who was a little younger but docile. Cledwyn was accepted as reliable as well as large, and Mrs Price explained that the Welsh band was noisy but not unduly aggressive. The whole thing could be regarded as a modern extension of folk singing and older people had to accommodate themselves with youthful high spirits. What she could not know was that a small gang of youths from Bangor were out looking for trouble. Cledwyn and Cyril got caught in the middle of a street battle. Cledwyn knew his way around back streets and managed to escape, but Cyril was stabbed and left bleeding on the ground. Even when the ambulance arrived the paramedics were attacked and the police had to move in before poor Cyril could be rushed to hospital.

Katica was distraught. I had never seen a woman tear her hair out before. Mrs Price was sullen with guilt and Cledwyn slunk around with the weight of the world on his shoulders. It all became my business. I was elevated into the role of peacemaker. When catastrophes strike there is no time for reflection. They occur anywhere anytime in a split second, then leave you to spend the rest of your life wondering why they should have occurred; like worrying about the origins of the Universe.

I have put Cyril in the bedroom prepared for my grandson Gabriel. It is the best place for his convalescence. Katica can cluck over him like a mother hen without leaving work. Cledwyn comes here to play chess with his friend and run messages for him: carrying his schoolwork to and fro. I find myself engaged in the kind of diplomacy my father excelled in when dealing with disputatious deacons. It will be easier to persuade Katica to forgive Mrs Price than to get that proud shopkeeper to accept forgiveness. These things take time. Some kind of a household is forming, and in my own mind I can call Henefail, and the village and this ancient sprawling parish, home.

The Ring and the Book

'WELL now. I'll leave you two dear people together,' the director's assistant said.

She spoke as though there was much for her to attend to. She was a smart, bright young thing, conspicuously so at the Riviera Residential Home for the Elderly. If asked, she always said she loved her job. The Home was a noble establishment among landscaped gardens, tucked away off a cul de sac with a distant view of the Mediterranean and within walking distance of a nice little shopping centre. It was surrounded by a high wall and trees and there was something or other in bloom all the year round and most of the elderly were calm and comfortable with loads of accommodation; and if they were not there was a staff of carers and nurses, and English was the spoken language of the Home, and her French was good enough to get by – so what more could a young unattached female ask for?

'I'm sure you have such a lot to say to each other.'

Raymond shuffled to his feet. He was tall and rather bent over and, as his sister Rosamund put it, as thin as a whittled stick. She remained seated, plump, powdered, prosperous, an exemplary resident, with many rings on her fingers.

167

'Unless of course you would like some tea?'

There was some polite dumb show before both declined and the young woman bustled out. It was a beautiful autumn afternoon and through the long windows residents could be seen moving about in the garden sunlight or sitting in the shade. For the time being, sister and brother had the Common Room to themselves. The quiet suggested each was waiting for the other to speak first. There was no denying a degree of estrangement. Raymond's wife Sybil had dubbed Rosamund's husband, Victor, 'a commercial conman' and Rosamund had found that unforgivable. In return, Victor and Rosamund had called Sybil a 'snob' and a 'culture vulture'. Raymond was distressed by it all and deeply regretted what he called 'entrenched positions', but there was very little he could do about it. He took refuge, and consolation, in his theatrical adventures. But now Sybil was dead, Victor had died long ago, and brother and sister were not exactly shipwrecked on life's further shore, but both widowed, isolated and drawn together towards the end to be closer to what they had been at the beginning. As Raymond saw it, childhood and old age had come together for an ultimate encounter. All that came between, more than sixty years, needed to dwindle to a vanishing point.

Rosamund was ten years older, doting on her little brother. They were evacuees together, tucked away in Glanaber, the family holiday home on Anglesey, above Traeth Coch where the ebb line revealed a stretch of sand two miles wide, and the high tide would erode the foreshore, leaving a network of grassy earth islands, where little Raymond, blue eyed and with golden curls, could leap about giving the islands the names of countries and continents. His imagination never ceased to delight her. Her bicycle was bigger than his and she would circle around to make sure he did not stray beyond the incoming tide. His piping voice and excited cries were carried on the wind like the calling of sea birds. She was in charge and he was so trusting and cheerful and good-natured.

Their mother rarely came out of Glanaber. She was stricken with ill health and self-pity, forever moaning the loss of a plantation in Malaya, which was her inheritance. 'We lost absolutely everything,' she would intone at the first opportunity. She needed sympathy more than children. Father was away from home, his factory of bathroom ware and household fittings diverted to urgent war effort, and when he visited, he would tease his wife by saying she sounded like something out of Somerset Maugham. 'You've got nothing to complain about,' he would say, 'living in this oasis of tranquillity, while the world is tearing itself to bits.' He made dire predictions about the end of Empire and the children invented endless games they could play on the shore. When the wind blew, as it so often did, they made paper kites, and it warmed her with happiness to watch little Raymond dashing about. And now he was this worn, thin creature sitting in front of her and they were contemplating a conversation like strangers in a train.

'You look very comfortable here. A nice place?'

He was the first to speak and to venture a friendly smile.

'So far, so good,' she said.

'I was thinking of Glanaber,' he said. 'Happy days.'

'Happy days indeed.'

Rosamund bowed her head in regal concession. The happy days were all very well, but there had been other days that had been far from happy. The name, Glanaber, for her, had not retained the talismanic quality it clearly had for him. It marked the first serious breach in their relationship. She and dear Victor had been married barely a year and he was badly in need of a break from his strenuous efforts to restore the family business. He needed to take a deep breath of those refreshing breezes before initiating the next phase of expansion... and what did they find? One of those black spots that mark the passage of time.

Glanaber was already occupied by Raymond and an awful actress named Meleri something, whom Raymond was besotted with. That was not the worst of it. The girl was recovering from an abortion and her brother was not responsible, for goodness sake. The man in question was a leading man as famous as anything in those days, with a name, which she had made a strenuous effort to forget, emblazoned brazenly outside a certain theatre in the West End. The foolish boy did everything for her, and then she flew off and the Lord alone knew where she had landed. She gave up her stage ambitions and married a lord. That's what Rosamund had heard. They lived somewhere abroad in luxurious anonymity. Wherever it was she had broken the silly boy's heart and he had never been the same again. It was probably the emotional damage he had suffered that made him such easy prey for that vulture Sybil, who was much too old for him. Of course she had the money and she encouraged him in some of his more ridiculous adventures.

'Would you be wanting to retire there?' she said. 'No more theatrical adventures.'

There were several ways of interpreting the scorn in her smile and he knew them all. They went back a long way. At Cambridge Raymond had become obsessed with the theatre and decided to become an actor. It was too awful. The boy was overgrown and gangling and he had never learned to speak properly. He had developed a silly habit of whispering under his breath, as if everything he said was some aesthetical revelation, and he'd never really grown out of it. It was all she could do to restrain herself from some reprimand about it now, before anybody turned up and they would need to raise their voices. Father was appalled and so was Victor, the handsome Hungarian refugee who was transforming the business at a time when it surely needed transforming. Father was too rooted, bogged down Victor said, in pre-war custom and practice. All was poised to expand on a grand scale and there was a place reserved for Raymond. Instead he dropped out before graduating and joined a miserable Repertory Company in Eastbourne. The silly boy found satisfaction knitting in the wings while waiting for his cue to go on playing a butler at least twice his age. Father's strength was failing and it seemed inevitable

Rosamund should marry Victor. That might not have happened if Raymond had joined the firm. Not that Victor was a bad husband. Far from it. But he was pushing forty when they married and she might have married somebody younger. And of course he had a Past. Who didn't at that time, and at that age?

'Retire!' he said. 'Yes I suppose it's time I thought about it.'

He restrained himself from a prolonged whisper on the theme that old theatre men never retired only faded away.

'I could do worse than Glanaber couldn't I? That blessed retreat from the world's alarms.'

'I've no idea what it's worth,' Rosamund said. 'I expect it needs a lot doing to it. You could always sell it and book yourself a place down here.'

'It's half yours, Ros. I wouldn't do anything without your approval, would I?'

It pleased her to hear him call her 'Ros'. After all there was no-one else left who would do it. But it was a bit much hearing him talk about 'her approval'. Raymond had been no great shakes as an actor, but he blossomed forth as an impresario. Or at least he did until Sybil came along. His enthusiasm and unselfish dogged devotion brought success to a number of West End shows. Writers, directors and particularly actors enjoyed working with him. The spectacle of this tall, thin man advancing towards them in rehearsal rubbing his hands together and whispering streams of admiring comments that they only half understood, warmed all their hearts. At first, that Sybil was so ingratiating. She had aristocratic connections and she had a way of dropping illustrious names that did not at all seem like name dropping. It was an oblique skill and Rosamund had admired it. It certainly impressed Victor to the extent of being one of four guarantors of a Shakespearean tour of Eastern Europe that proved ruinously expensive. This was all Sybil's fault. She planned the itinerary and the company found themselves in towns where scarcely anyone understood English simply because she wanted to visit some obscure archaeological site. And an unsympathetic creature too. When some spiteful competitor spread a rumour that Victor had collaborated with the Germans during the war, the family should have rallied around to defend his good name. They owed it to him. It was the least they could do. Instead that sinister Sybil made sure that Raymond was unavailable when his sister most needed him. It was unforgivable. It gave rise to an estrangement that lasted many years. She was gone now, but it was still hard for Rosamund to forgive. She could best cope with her brother now by being sorry for him. He was basically weak as well as being naïve. She had to make an effort to remember how loving and trusting he had been as a child. Perhaps she herself should take some of the blame for having spoilt him? That was possible.

A frail old woman with abundant white hair propelled herself on her spindle-thin legs into the centre of the Common Room as if she were late for an appointment. She stood stock-still to study the brother and sister sitting opposite each other across the low table. She stared at them with frank, blue-eyed curiosity. She pointed a finger at Raymond, who seemed to think he ought to offer her his chair. Rosamund placed a restraining hand on his arm.

'Ill met by moonlight, proud Titania!'

Her voice was clear and surprisingly youthful. Having delivered the line she lost interest in the visitor and began to wander around the room in search of something she seemed to have lost.

'She's not supposed to be in here,' Rosamund said.

A burly woman in white nurse's uniform appeared. She had prominent teeth and appeared to be constantly smiling.

'Now Millie dear, we shouldn't be in here, should we now...'

She spoke with a distinct Scottish accent. She had her own way of exercising her authority. Her arms were out-stretched to offer guidance and direction in case the patient were to collapse under the burden of her frailty. In fact the old woman called Millie was surprisingly agile. They made a circle of the Common Room like children playing an indoor game.

'It's my ring,' the old woman said. 'I've lost my ring. I've got to find it.'

'Of course we'll find it, Millie dear. Of course we will.'

They trotted out the way they had come in. Their voices could be heard drifting down a corridor, agitated and soothing by turn. Rosamund looked at her brother. He appeared unduly disturbed.

'She knew me,' he said.

'Of course she didn't,' Rosamund said. 'She's like that with every visitor if she gets the chance. Not that she does get a chance all that often. She's an inmate of another part of this establishment. Another part of the forest.'

Rosamund was prepared to take the incident lightly. They had far more important family matters to discuss. Her brother remained agitated.

'The awful thing is, I think I know her.'

'You think she could have been an actress?' she said. 'Just because she quotes Shakespeare. Even I remember that bit from school.'

'Excuse me.'

Raymond was on his feet.

'I must find out more about her.'

'Oh really!' Rosamund said, 'your imagination.'

He ignored her insistence that he should sit down.

At reception he found the director's assistant seated at a computer screen some way behind the counter. He shifted the visitor's book to one side with his elbow and coughed politely to attract her attention. She was quick to her feet ready with a smiling response.

'That little old lady, wandering about,' Raymond said.

'Such a sweet creature,' the young woman said.

She was smiling as though to demonstrate she herself shared the same quality.

'Quite harmless really. She has a lovely nature. And we think she is very well connected. I know she has a title. Lady something. She was here before I arrived. We call her 'Millie' and she seems to like that. After all we are all the same in the end, aren't we?'

'I think I know her,' Raymond said.

'Do you really? How interesting…'

The tone of voice also suggested how potentially awkward. The smile was still there, but her grip tightened on the propelling pencil in her hands.

'She was saying something about losing a ring.'

'Oh the ring…'

The young woman relaxed a little.

'Sometime it's the crown as well, but we think that must be Shakespeare. Usually it's the ring. We keep it here.'

She opened a drawer under the counter and produced a gold ring with a single small diamond.

'It's nothing very special, but it means an awful lot to Millie obviously. Her little hands are so thin it keeps falling off. We always find it before the day is done. So she wears it going to bed and nurse says she sleeps like an angel.'

'Could I see it?'

'Yes of course.'

With the ring between his trembling fingers Raymond moved to the doorway so that he could examine it in the bright sunlight. He could make out an inscription, two names and a knot symbol. Meleri & Raymond. Still clutching the ring in his fist, he sank into a deep leather chair in the reception area like a man exhausted after a journey. With his head lowered and his eyes screwed up he saw Mahmood the watchmaker in his tiny crowded shop in the alley off

Hammersmith Grove engraving the letters inside the ring.

This was the day when Meleri told him she was pregnant and he so gallantly said it would make no difference. It was she who insisted on having an abortion. For the sake of her career. And it was he who insisted they should escape to Glanaber where she could recover. 'Regroup' was the cheerful word he had used. He could hear it now. And he had remained unremittingly cheerful for the whole period, until she insisted on going away and making a fresh start. He had been heartbroken, 'devastated' would be the current word, until Sybil came along and the whole tragic episode was blotted out of his consciousness by the force of her powerful personality. It had no more reality than an alcoholic dream; but now the thoughts were facts, as substantial as the ring clutched in his hand.

'Are you all right?'

The director's assistant expressed her concern. She was uncertain whether to leave her side of the counter and get closer to the bent length of the thin man in the leather chair.

'Can I get you something?' she said. 'Should I go and call your sister?'

He shook his head and raised a hand to restrain the young woman. He murmured something about being all right in a minute.

'Just a bit of a shock,' he said. 'That's all.'

But was it? Coincidences could be like earthquakes, you could never anticipate them: only once they happened they took on the mantle of inevitability, rather like the course of history, always there, waiting to be explained, waiting to be given a meaning. What did this mean? He was a man at the end of a career in the theatre, waiting and wondering what on earth he should do next. He had always seen himself as a man with a mission. This had driven him through all the vicissitudes of a career with as many ups and downs as a figure eight at a fair. His pulse was racing as he considered the possibility of a new chapter beginning: a fresh start even. He could hear the voices approaching again. Millie appeared to be in flight from her benevolent captor.

'Millie dear. It will be eating time soon. Let's get back to our rooms, shall we? There's a lovely programme on the television. All about red squirrels. You know how you love them.'

'I must find my ring.'

She seemed well aware she would find the ring somewhere in the region of the reception area. She stood still to look up at the tall man who confronted her, her eyes dashing about filled with fear and suspicion.

'Who are you?' she said. 'What do you want?'

'Meleri.'

He spoke the name as tenderly as he could. He repeated it.

'Raymond,' he said. 'Glanaber. Long ago.'

She was shaking her head. He opened his hand so that she could see the ring.

'I'm Raymond,' he said. 'I gave you this ring. You can read our names inside it.'

She turned to her nurse who advanced to put her arms around her. She needed support.

'That's my ring,' she said. 'What's this man doing with it? He's stolen it.'

'Meleri. Meleri. I gave you this ring. Don't you remember?'

'I want my ring back.'

The patient was getting increasingly agitated.

'Better you give it her,' the nurse urged in her quietest voice. Once the ring was on her finger, the frail woman calmed down. She straightened up ready to adopt a role.

'Set this down, that one may smile and smile, and be a villain…'

'Now come along, Millie dear. We've got such a lot to do.'

Clutching the ring on her finger, meekly enough, Millie allowed herself to be led away. Raymond collapsed into the deep leather chair and held his head in his hands. Alarmed, the director's assistant rushed to the Common Room to inform Rosamund of her brother's distressed condition. Rosamund rose to her feet with some difficulty. As she said herself she had reached a stage when she much preferred sitting down to walking. The Home provided routine consultations with a doctor and he had recommended that Rosamund should take more exercise. She did so grudgingly. And she did not take kindly to her brother staging an emotional collapse on his first visit. Whatever ghost from the past he imagined he had seen, she had no intention of taking the young woman into her confidence about it. It seemed to her the most appropriate way of dealing with this crisis was to ask the director's assistant to provide them with more tea in a sheltered corner of the south terrace. It was within easy reach and should not cause the busy young woman undue trouble.

'Could you be so kind...'

She was a thoughtful, understanding girl and Rosamund would commend her to the director when he returned. She was a woman already pledged to endow the establishment on her demise: so she would have the best attention when she needed it.

'She didn't recognise me,' he said. 'She had no idea who I was.'

Rosamund maintained a disapproving silence. She restrained herself from telling Raymond not to moan about it. For goodness sake, with all the years that had gone by and after so many exploits and goodness knows indescribable adventures there was no good reason why she should remember. And there was no need for Raymond to make such a tragedy out of it either. Through all the years when Sybil dominated his life he had not so much mentioned the wretched Meleri. And if she by some magic process had become the harmless Millie it had to be some form of improvement.

'The poor thing has gone quite ga-ga,' she said. 'You do realise that, don't you?'

'Yes, I suppose so,' he said. 'But it's so strange. Life can be so pitiless. So tragic. I'm shaken, you know. Really, shaken.'

A pair of resident dowagers appeared walking arm in arm along the path that led to a wall covered in bougainvillea. They greeted Rosamund.

'Such a beautiful afternoon.'

She nodded graciously. They may have been curious about the visitor. Rosamund had no intention of introducing Raymond to anyone in his present emotional state. The way of life in a residential home had to be a stately ceremony, otherwise the entire fabric would fall to pieces.

'I think we ought to keep quiet about it,' she said. 'After all I have to go on living here. A place like this can easily be reduced to a hive of gossip. Especially among the staff.'

'I'm sorry.'

Raymond emerged from the depths to become aware of his sister's displeasure and distress.

'It's such a shame you've been upset in this way. It's most unfortunate.'

Raymond apologised again.

'I was so looking forward to talking to you about family matters.'

'Yes of course.'

He straightened up making a visible attempt to pull himself together. Here and now, the sunlight and shade they shared in this moment in time made it the only moment that mattered; that demanded his whole attention. Brother and sister were bound together in family matters.

'Glanaber,' he said. 'I wouldn't do anything without consulting you, Ros.'

'There's something I haven't told you about before. I was hoping to ask you to help.'

'Well of course, Ros, of course.'

'Dear Victor wrote an autobiography.'

'Did he really?'

Raymond struggled to display genuine interest. Victor had never been dear to him and it must be at least thirteen years since he died. There had been times when he treated Raymond with open contempt, 'the man's buried up to his neck in candy-floss' – and between Victor and Sybil there had been passages of snarling open warfare, the memory of which still distressed him. But de mortuis nihil nisi bonum or words to that effect. It was quite possible he had a lot to justify.

'I never told you about it and I was never sure whether he meant it for publication. Perhaps not. When he was writing it there were all those books pouring out about spies and the third and the fourth and the fifth man. He said if he did get it published it would be trampled to death in the stampede. In his own way you know Victor was a very cultured man. He gave up a lot to put the family business back on its feet.'

Raymond bowed his long neck. It could have been a gesture of repentance, although as far as he could recall, Victor gave up nothing and gained a lot.

'I brought it with me here. I told the director about it. He was very charming and helpful. He always is. But he does have a habit of disappearing. I was hoping to introduce you. Anyway he had a friend in publishing and he got him to read it. I parted with it for months and then eventually back it came with a note saying it was very interesting although it needed polishing because Victor's literary style wasn't very good; but it would never get published because Victor was not famous enough. I was really hurt.'

'Yes, of course. Of course you were.'

'As though the sacrifices of little people didn't count. And Victor made enormous sacrifices.'

Even when he first heard the account all of forty years ago it had been difficult to disentangle fact from fantasy. It may have been true that he had collaborated with an Austrian Nazi official to get both his aunts, who were half Jewish, visas to travel to Switzerland and safety. But had he really slipped into Yugoslavia to join the Partisans and had he really blown up a bridge with a couple of German tanks on it? Sybil was always scathingly sceptical. But Sybil was dead and gone and Rosamund was sitting in front of him alive with intentions.

'What I thought was...' Rosamund said. 'You have a fine command of English. I don't know whether the idea appeals to you at all. If you could edit it, I would get it privately printed. There are those small, specialised fine arts people who could produce a very limited edition. Say a hundred copies.'

He was touched by her eagerness. There were after all deep reservoirs of residual affection between them that had been buried deep in the sand of the intervening years. For a moment he had a glimpse of his big sister suggesting a new game they could play along the foreshore at Traeth Coch.

'You could have Glanaber,' she said. 'Set yourself up there for a few months. Peace and quiet. Nice and warm. Do you think you could do it?'

Raymond summoned up all his resources of goodwill.

'Yes of course, Ros,' he said. 'Of course I'll do it.'

183

The Garden Cottage

'OF course I look old,' Sir Robin said, fingering his long smoky beard. 'I am old. But nobody is born old. Nobody is young forever either. Except in legends. That's why we like myths and legends so much.'

The married couple were soothed, made at ease, and even quietly flattered by the close attention the old gentleman was paying them. He was tall and very thin and showing off a little but he was entitled to do so as he paced in his own sprightly fashion around his own kitchen. They knew more about him than he could possibly know about them; but even then what they knew was very little, and Anna, a native so to speak, was especially eager to learn more. Her husband, Idris, was pleased to be in the cool. Outside, as they walked, they had been overtaken by the sudden heat of early summer and he had been uncomfortable in unsuitable city clothes. The collar and tie were still too tight and his best course was to sit still and listen politely in the cool of the large kitchen.

'Myths and legends precede stories. I'm quite sure of that. To my own satisfaction anyway. Just as stories precede fiction. And why is that?'

He paused just long enough to sense that they were equally interested in the question. He could see the couple were smiling at each other in a way that suggested they were still pleased in what they saw after twenty-five years of marriage.

'As with everything else,' Sir Robin said, 'the answer is in ourselves not in our stars. If I may say so, you both look supremely blessed in each other. You saw all the flowers in the cottage garden blazing away. And you stopped to admire them, who wouldn't? But why today, I wonder? More tea perhaps?'

He was a significant figure from the past, Sir Robin Williams Price the last, the very last of the Williams Prices of Plas Gilwern, making them welcome in the kitchen extension of the Gardener's Cottage, which, with all its modernised conveniences and flourishing garden, was what he had left. The lane they had walked down led to the Home Farm which he had sold long ago in a vain attempt to balance the books. The Plas itself was now an upmarket old people's home, approached from the west side of the park, which was also no longer his.

The couple glanced at each other shyly; deciding which of them should speak first. Idris had the protruding belly that went with good food and a sedentary occupation. His hair was thin but he still had a charming smile and was wont to tuck in his stomach and mutter it was time he took up squash again. Anna was dark with dimples and, as her husband would say, still a marvellously good-looking woman.

'It's an anniversary,' she said at last. 'Anniversary of the day we first met.'

'Well there you are!'

Sir Robin beamed, a tall, thin, bearded figure with a teapot in his large hands. They had to be cheered by the way he looked pleased for them.

'You are legend, you are history! That is delightful. You mean you met here? On this very spot?'

'My great aunt lived here, Mrs Hughes. The head gardener's wife. That must have been in your father's time, I expect?'

Anna was hesitant because of the smoky beard. Sprightly as he was, could their host be even older than he looked? And how much of the old days would he wish to be reminded of?

'Old Mrs Hughes,' he said, 'well I never. Such a wonderful old woman. I remember her well, I'm ashamed to say. Ashamed, I suppose that's the word. Old Hughes went for the best part of a year unpaid. It was his idea. He said they could live on the produce since they paid no rent. This was in the early thirties when things were really bad. A wonderful man, Old Hughes. And she was a wonderful woman.'

Anna was encouraged by the warmth of his recollection. She could be proud of her ancient relatives. In their day they had been staunch, loyal and proud.

'I used to bring her eggs and butter and cakes,' she said. 'From Bronant, our farm. And at this time of the year I would leave loaded with flowers.'

'Bronant,' he said. 'Freehold. Very good farm.'

Then he pointed playfully at Idris.

'And one fine day, your prince arrived? Did he?'

After a slight hesitation Idris decided to enter into the spirit of the occasion. It was a bit odd, but after all it could be part of what they came for. A kind of celebration.

'I was on holiday at Home Farm.'

'Well I never. The Harvey Joneses was it?'

'John Harvey Jones was my uncle. Or at least my mother's first cousin.'

'But you weren't a local boy, were you? A young city gent enjoying his hols in the country?'

Sir Robin pressed his unexpected guests to take more tea and cakes.

'I saw this lovely girl wobbling along on her bike, her arm full of flowers!'

'So of course you had to help. And that was the beginning of it all. What an enchanting story. And you are still... how shall I put it? You must tell me all!'

He popped the best part of a scone in his mouth, and such was his eagerness to hear their story, he didn't bother to close it as he chewed. His long teeth looked rather loose and he covered his mouth with his hand. The happy couple looked at each other and made polite allowances. Once he had the masticating process under control, Sir Robin pressed on with his enquiries.

'The path of true love never did run smooth, or did it? Obviously it did. Here you are. In the selfsame cottage looking blissfully happy. It was meant to happen. Like a legend. Therefore it was ordained. And we have to be grateful. But grateful to whom? Or even to what? You know that is a question that has bothered me all my life. I've always felt everything that ever happened to me was more or less my own fault. But in the case of other people, better people? Maybe you can provide an answer? That would be wonderful. Tell me all.'

His enthusiasm was enough to cool and curb Idris, who began to look uncomfortable.

'There isn't really all that much to tell.'

Anna responded more positively. This was after all Sir Robin, the last of the Williams Prices of Plas Gilwern, only the most notable family for miles around, taking an interest.

'Oh, but yes there is,' she said. 'You've no idea, Sir Robin.'

'Robin will do,' the knight said amiably.

Anna took a deep breath and smiled to show she was greatly encouraged.

'It wasn't all romance. Far from it. Idris had a hard struggle. Really hard. His father worked on the railway. Killed in an awful accident. His mother kept a corner shop in Hounslow, but the Asians arrived from Uganda and put her out of business. Idris had to leave school and work in Sainsbury's filling shelves. My parents didn't want me to have anything to do with him. But he went to night school and the manager recommended him to the Midland and he worked his way up and now he's deputy regional director of securities and investments in Wales and the South West. We live in Cardiff.'

191

'But that's wonderful,' Sir Robin said. 'You must be proud of him.'

'Oh, I am.'

Menopause or no, the slight flush was becoming. This was the young girl loaded with flowers, the same disarming smile and peerless skin. All the same Idris resented having his career squeezed into one breathless squawk in front of what was, at least as far he was concerned, a complete stranger.

'I should have met him years ago,' Sir Robin was saying. 'Nothing I needed more in those days than an intelligent banker. I'm afraid our local man was a bigger idiot than I was, which is saying something.'

Or was he? Idris took a professional glimpse into the past and saw an embarrassed bank manager trying to cope with a fractious would-be country gentleman with more pretensions than money; an historic relic with dwindling assets. It could have been a mistake to call at the gardener's cottage. Anna's ancient aunt was long deceased and the hedgerows on either side of the narrow road that led down to the beach had been shorn down to what he called 'suburban proportions'. This wasn't the delightful countryside he had explored when staying at the Home Farm. There were hedges then that were slightly uneven, and when he borrowed a cousin's bike to go out to meet Anna, they cast enticing shadows across the road on a day like this and added mystery and adventure to their secret trips as well as concealment. You never knew when the foreshore would come into view, or whether the tide was in or out. Now, on a blazing day like this, you could see too much, the landscape was too exposed and there was no shade anywhere, which was why Anna insisted on calling at the cottage to ask for a glass of water and now they were exposed to this.

'And you have a family of course?'

Anna was swept away by the elegant way he asked, as if he were begging the most enormous favour.

'A girl and two boys,' she said.

'Delightful,' Sir Robin said, plainly eager to know more.

'Alice works at Goldman Sachs. Gained a Two One in Maths. Two more marks and it would have been a First. She has a partner, as they call it nowadays. Hans. A very nice boy. Alwyn is completing his first year at Jesus College, Oxford. He's a very wild Welshman. The Dafydd ap Gwilym and so on. Arfon is still at school. Mad on rugby. Thinks of nothing else. Idris wants him to do law. We shall see, shan't we?'

'Marvellous,' Sir Robin said.

At last Anna had sensed her husband's disapproval and the stream of triumphant information suddenly dried. Sir Robin stroked his long beard as though he were calculating a small sum.

'Alice, Alwyn and Arfon. And your surname begins with A, Mr and Mrs Adams. What should we say? Top of the list. Nothing but the best. And why not? Absolutely splendid.'

The best thing was to laugh. A good laugh establishes an atmosphere of goodwill. For Anna it was a relief. Idris was capable of putting on a frosty, almost hostile, front the moment he felt the occasion warranted it. Part of his training, she assumed, in the bank. Idris made an effort to relax. All the same, when it did come out, it did sound rather like a bank manger questioning a client.

'Sir Robin,' he said. 'How long is it since you lived in the Plas?'

He added in a less inquisitorial tone: 'Such a charming old manor house. Late seventeenth century, would it be?'

'Oh, years and years,' Sir Robin said vaguely. He raised both hands to feel the back of his neck. 'I might have caused an occlusion, laughing so much.'

The word sounded distinctly medical. Anna showed sympathy and concern.

'Much too conscious of my skeleton these days,' he said. 'I suppose it comes of being so thin. It's all I've got left. The connection between my spine and my cortex. It's not the time of year, of course, but even on a fine day like this, I see it like a solitary cabbage stalk with a mangy green head standing all alone in a bare windswept field. Pretty awful that. I mean disrespectful of the blessings of nature. My poor Marcia always said I was not bodily grounded.'

The tone had become more light-hearted with the mention of his wife's name. Anna's lips were parted. She had a vague recollection of a Lady Marcia Williams Price who had been regarded as a formidable presence even in rumour.

'She was a Czech national you know. Sudeten-deutsch. Her family were in the Almanac de Gotha for heaven's sake. *Erste gesellschaft* and all that. Enough to keep them going during the Nazi occupation. But didn't save them from the

Commies. They had to skidaddle from Czechoslovakia in 1948, all the jewels and family heirlooms in a couple of suitcases. In those days back in the fifties, there was still a network of country houses around. Even butlers. We still had a butler. And a pretty good wine cellar from my father's time. They were able to get Marcia into Roedean. She was christened 'Marguerite' by the way, but she was already 'Marcia' by the time I met her. Strange isn't it? People still thought of themselves as 'well born' in those days. Of course bags of jewels don't last forever. The sixties blew all that sort of thing away, just after we were married. We weren't really equipped to deal with all the equalitarian pressure around. No education. We'd been brought up to believe we were the best by right of birth, which was rubbish of course. Nothing worse than impoverished country squires. Dabbling in this and that and succeeding in nothing.'

'You had family?'

Idris Adams tried to sound sympathetic. At least it was cool in the kitchen. It would be a long walk in the heat of the afternoon to where they had left his BMW. He would have liked to have learned more about the wine cellar. He took a lot of interest in wine. It was an interesting topic of conversation with important clients.

'Two delightful little girls, Lucy and Lilly. I still like thinking of them as little poppets. Awful isn't it? Old men dwell too much in the past. Well of course they do. There isn't anywhere much else where they can go to. You may remember Lilly?'

He put the question to Anna who frowned hard with the effort of sympathetic recollection.

'Well of course not. You are much too young. One so easily forgets how frightfully old one is. We sent the girls to the local grammar, or was it comprehensive by then? Not just to avoid expense. Marcia was terribly keen we should integrate with the local population. That was the way she put it, until I said the Williams Prices had been here since before the flood. We weren't intruders for goodness sake. Well there you are then, she said. And she packed me off for two successive years to a summer school in Harlech to brush up on my Welsh. The trouble was I didn't have all that much to brush up. We have a Harpist's Room, she said. Your great-great-grandfather used to employ a harpist. So what kind of a mongrel are you? I'm not very good at languages, I said, but I'm very good with sheep and cattle. I spoke too soon of course. My pedigree herd was wiped out by foot and mouth.'

'How terrible.'

Idris was deeply sympathetic. He was ready to draw upon his own experience of valued clients who had been visited with the same plague. Sir Robin was deeply immersed now in his retrospection. It was as though he had much to confess or at least to get off his chest.

'You understand the anxieties of parenthood?'

'Oh, we do, indeed.'

Idris and Anna were in complete agreement. Had they not graduated from romantic lovers to responsible parents?

'Poor Marcia. As the girls grew up she started to revert to type. All that antediluvian stuff about the marriage market among the central European aristocracy. Our estate was going downhill fast and she thought part of the answer would be to get the girls well married. And since they were mad on horses we had to do all we could to encourage them. Dressage, show jumping, point to point and polo, all that sort of thing. Ruinously expensive. It wasn't cattle or sheep that did the damage in the end. It was those damned horses!'

A heavy silence descended on the kitchen. Sir Robin looked troubled, like a man who still had momentous decisions to make. There was no easy way whereby the married couple could take leave. In any case Anna was too spellbound to move. Idris considered making a helpful comment. After all, he had conquered adversity and was entitled to the authority of a moderately successful man.

'You were the victim of social and economic forces, Sir Robin,' he said.

He was prepared to elaborate but it would take time to marshal a more precise analysis. The old man was looking at him as if for the first time he had realised that he was entertaining a complete stranger in his kitchen. He had started some kind of an explanation; the woman was listening intently so he may as well finish it.

'The remedy was worse than the disease,' he said. 'What a pair of sons-in-law. A social-climbing property developer from Banbury and an Argentinian polo player who claimed he had a ranch near Cordoba which he couldn't touch because of political difficulties. They didn't get on at all but Lilly and Lucy stuck to each other like glue so they had to form fours. It was all about winning and even more about losing. Grooms and trainers and horse transport and bloodstock improvement. It drove us insane over the years. King Lear had three daughters. We only had two. Perhaps we should have had a third. Was there a Mrs Lear? Poor Marcia tore herself apart trying to please her daughters and all they did was turn on her in the end.'

The married couple could no nothing except share an appalled silence that took on the nature of a vigil.

'It's so good of you to listen to me.'

All the energy had gone out of Sir Robin's voice.

'There's never enough time is there? There are no clocks in legends. Only in Testaments. Three in the afternoon. The third day. The moment of truth. What will survive of what we had between us? It has to be love. But you don't really know even that, do you? Would you like to see her?'

The couple looked troubled and confused.

'She's lying on the dining-room table. Empty as an effigy. The dining table we don't use anymore. It's cool in there. We have flowers in there rooted in darkness. She's surrounded by flowers. They glow in the dark.'

Outside they heard the sound of tyres on the gravel.

'That will be the ambulance and the police. A little late in fact.'

Sir Robin sounded more cheerful.

'You've no idea how old people live inside the structure of the social services. Like weevils in wood. I've been expecting them all afternoon. Instead you called. I'm glad of that.'

He smiled benignly at their bowed heads.

Three Old Men

THE idea was to celebrate Peter Pritchard's eightieth birthday. True it had already occurred but, since the three of us had been in school together, a week or two late was neither here nor there. We were comrades in survival and a little more that that. All those years ago, Augustus Jones, our headmaster, a man given to bouts of enthusiasm, had declared in public that Tom Philips, Roderick Roberts and Peter Pritchard were the best and brightest pupils he had ever had. No doubt a misguided burst of hyperbole, but it stayed with us down the years, sank into an undercurrent of rivalry that seems to have coloured if not dominated our relationship. We should have been friends, perhaps, just for the sake of being friends, not runners pacing each other on a long distance race. We went our separate ways: myself into development via architecture; Rod into medicine and surgery, and Peter, more unusually, into acting. We kept in regular touch to enjoy our minor triumphs en route, and kept our disappointments to ourselves. The record never required we should be confessing to one another. There has to be a little glitter to our progress. There was always an unspecified goal. It has turned out to be old age.

We have survived the journey through the minefield of accidents and ailments. In my own case I have taken life to be an extendable present rather than an accumulation of numbers on the scoreboard. I have done well and I have much to be thankful for. ('Thankful to whom?' says Rod, who always had a sceptical nature. 'If you believe that, you can believe anything,' was another of his early dicta.) I pop into the office of Philips & Partners twice a week and play nine holes of golf on a Thursday afternoon. Rod is no longer an eminent surgeon and lives in comfortable retirement in a substantial cottage outside Llandeilo, free at last from recurring marital entanglements. Disappointments, like bereavements, never go away but lose their sting down the years. Peter's career, as one might expect, was more colourful and roller-coaster. He was acknowledged quite early on to be a fine theatre director and later a great classical actor, but he made his money in films, and in particular horror films. His huge eyes, beetle brows, hooked nose and that mellow baritone that easily acquired its touch of menace proved to be greater assets than his intelligence. He married his agent, Maggie Pryce, a tough woman who turned out to have an umbilical attachment to her birthplace in Ynys Môn. We incline to think this had been intensified by having spent several unhappy years in New York. In any case they bought and converted a farmhouse above Penmon with a walled garden and spectacular views of Eryri and the Menai Straits. Sadly, before they had settled in, Maggie was stricken with cancer. Rod and I made a big effort to attend the funeral, but Peter was so bent with grief he barely noticed we were present. He retreated to the farm, weighed down by his cruel fate. He determined to fulfil the dream they had of creating a library and a garden. They would become Maggie's memorial. He gave up acting and films and the theatre, he said, to devote himself to philosophical studies. With the passage of time his horror films became cult items, so that he acquired what he described as 'posthumous fame' and his retreat kept him out of an unwelcome limelight. He had to avoid the attentions of marauding fan clubs, especially during the tourist season.

I made what might be called the birthday party arrangements. I am not sure why, in the matter of reunions, this should invariably be the case. Perhaps because the other two see me as a businessman. Rod always had a streak of lazy indifference and in the operating theatre he was the centre of a little universe waited on, literally, hand and foot. Peter left everything to Maggie and after her death became chronically unworldly. Maybe I was the one with the most developed sense of social responsibility since I became a developer! I would like to think so. As I get older I have this need to justify my actions or at least explain them. What is it that inclined me to want to share my good fortune with my friends; or should I be more judicial and confess a desire to use my good fortune to transform a hidden rivalry into a more enduring friendship?

On arrival at the Trefarthen Country House Hotel, Rod and I presented ourselves at reception. We were confronted by an exceptionally good-looking Polish girl. I noticed Rod straighten up and brighten visibly. Still the ladies' man after two messy marriages and losing all his outstanding crop of fair hair. The beautiful Pole ignored his covetous smile and gave me all her cool professional attention. Rod was quite put out and I had to restrain myself from chuckling aloud. As we mounted the broad staircase I hear him mutter crossly.

'That's it. When they look right through you as though you weren't there, that's the end of the line!'

I was left marvelling at the vagaries of human nature or at least the male of the species. I remembered how moody Rod used to get when we witnessed Peter's invariable success with girls. He found it irritatingly unaccountable. After all, he, Roderick Roberts, was the acknowledged 'Handsome Harry', the captain of the first XV and the proud possessor of a fine head of fair wavy hair. There were unkind people who would describe Pritch as downright ugly. How he could exercise this magnetism among girls was not apparent to us, who were at an age when we knew the answer to everything. And now, seated around a table decorated with eight bright candles, in a private room in the well appointed Trefarthen Country House Hotel, with sauna available, we look at each other in uncomfortable silence, with a cold infinity of questions and no available answers.

The perfection of the arrangements intensified the silence. I wondered if Pritch saw ghosts from our common past parading behind our presence. He was looking ominously theatrical as ever. The fact was I had no idea what he could be thinking. Were we nothing more than old acquaintances masquerading as friends, old acquaintances with nothing to say to each other except repeating the word 'old'? Anxious as ever to the point of panic to observe the social niceties, I rehearsed the toast I already had in mind. My design was to neatly combine celebrating Pritch's eightieth with some reference to the memory of Augustus Jones MA who had for some unfathomable reason thought so highly of the three old men around the candlelit table when they were frisky untamed and unproven colts. I would refer to high points in Pritch's distinguished career and touch on corresponding peaks in Rod's and even mine. I was quite put out when Rod pushed back his chair and raised his glass. It was obvious he had already been drinking. The brief encounter with the receptionist's desk had clearly upset him.

'Here's looking at your ugly mug, Pritch old boy. Welcome to the Club! Decrepitude for ever!'

I had to join in the toast. Peter Pritchard was looking at us both as though he were struggling to remember where he had seen us before. He was slow on cue to respond and after he had done so he seemed to be absorbed in pursuing a train of thought that had been interrupted. I found his detachment disturbing. Did he not appreciate the effort I had made to arrange this special visit? Rod had slumped back in his chair and was prodding himself in the chest, absorbed in his own condition.

'I tell you something,' he said. 'You can take a little trip tomorrow to the nearest sand dunes and you can shoot me! You'd be doing me a favour. Very convenient. Easy to bury me in the sand.'

Was it a joke? It was hard to decide whether he was glaring at us or gloating. He was a doctor, and we had to accept he knew what he was talking about. He had always been short tempered but his professional reputation was high. Arab sheiks travelled long distances to be operated on by him.

'My useful life is over,' he said. 'I suppose it was useful. I hope I cured more people than I killed. I don't know who keeps the score. All that's left is to watch myself go ga ga. It's all there. Written in my arteries. And there's damn all I can do about it!'

I was quite hurt. Offended. I had gone out of my way in my new BMW to pick him up and bring him up here and I assumed he had enjoyed the trip. It was the middle of May and the weather was perfect and our native land looked like a green festival from one end to another. It was a time for celebration. The world was renewing itself and he seemed to be ignoring the fact that we were here to celebrate Pritch's birthday.

'Steady on, Rod,' I said. 'You're not the only one. We are all in the same boat. We think about these things too, you know. But it's now that matters. Now with a capital N. The world's here to educate us to the last moment. I can hear old Gussie saying it. And I'm sure the old windbag was right. He used to say the world is packed with wonders pining for recognition.'

I was rather pleased with dredging up those old saws for fresh recognition. Rod was unmoved.

'I've never been afraid to face facts. You'd be no bloody good in my job if you couldn't. You are as old as your arteries and that's the beginning and the end of it. When you're dead you're burned or buried and that's the end of it and good riddance. Of course most people, the vast majority, are willing and eager to be fobbed off with candy-floss. Maybe they have to be to keep the old social wheels oiled. But facts are facts and that's all there is to it.'

'Did you hear that, Pritch? The whole world of the arts and humanities dismissed in two words and a hyphen. Candy-floss. My goodness!'

I cheered up. At least we were arguing and that was better than staring at each other in embarrassed silence. Peter Pritchard held on to what I thought was a theatrical pause, those big eyes staring at us at their most mesmeric as they used to with an audience.

'You might consider,' Pritch said, 'you are reading the wrong script.'

He gave us both a broad benevolent smile.

'Wrong?'

The doctor poked himself in the chest.

'What else have I got to read except myself?'

Pritch rose to his feet and walked to the window. He pulled a theatrical face to show he was not pleased with what he saw. The hotel management had illuminated the gardens and trees until they were bathed in a romantic light.

'What bloody script are you talking about?'

Pritch raised both arms. He was going to declaim in style, which I welcomed. It would at least liven things up.

'This island has twenty-eight standing stones,' he said. 'Twenty-eight meini hirion. They have been standing there for three or four thousand years. What are they for? What do they mean? All sorts of theories have been canvassed. And discounted.'

'And now you've got one,' Rod said.

Pritch ignored the interruption. His mellow voice was edging towards incantation.

'You need to imagine this island as it was four thousand years ago. Long long before the Celts and their druids. What were they related to, these humans who lived and died here then? To the skies of course. To the stars. The stars were their books. Their constant illumination. The constellations were a language and those standing stones were there to read them. Perhaps more than read them. They were petrified avatars.'

'Goodness gracious. You have looked into it.'

Rod had settled to be more jovial than sarcastic, which was a relief, mellowed I hope by the excellent wine I had ordered and paid for.

'What's an avatar by the way?'

'Messengers from a higher level of consciousness,' Pritch said. 'That's one way of putting it. They can occur anywhere and anytime. But these standing stones are there for all time to teach each succeeding generation to look up and learn. To accept that they are privileged for their brief term to be at the centre of the universe.'

He created another pause.

'I've been thinking a lot about you two,' he said. 'How calm are you?'

To me it seemed he meant how calm were we in the face of our imminent extinction and I resented the question. It was like asking what answers you had given to those difficult questions in the exam that you had failed to answer.

'Maggie introduced me to meditation. It helps me anyway.'

'Jolly good.'

Rod raised his glass to drink his health and I did the same. It seemed the answer most immediately to hand.

'In this day and age,' Pritch said, 'we are so obsessed with ourselves we can't see very much else. But the Neolithic people, on this spot where I am standing now, were constantly aware of everything beyond them. And I would say the human race, human nature, has always been aware of this. Of higher states of consciousness related to higher states of being. Always. At least until it gave way to the satanic temptation that it could control the world. Master it. Subdue it. Bend it to the human will. No room for Avatars any more. Only for obedient robots. And egos bigger than atom bombs... now then. Tomorrow. I want to show you something. We need to start out bright and early and have the place to ourselves. And take our candles with us. So that we can read the Runes.'

And so it was, the following morning, bright and early, we set out in my roomy and comfortable BMW to cross to the other side of the island. As though they were maps, Pritch presented us with drawings of the decorated stones he wanted us to see. In the passenger seat, Rod nursed them disdainfully in his lap, making a half-hearted attempt to prevent them dropping under his feet.

'There we are,' Pritch said. 'Stone on stone transferred to pencil on paper. And photocopied of course. There you have three processes of transposing meaning into signs. Just what was spelt out by a stone chisel four thousand years ago? They knew what fragile creatures we are. Not like stone or stars.'

'Decorations can just be decorations,' Rod said. 'Prehistoric doodles. You have to find something to do when it's raining cats and dogs and there's no telly.'

'Lettering is only decoration until we are taught to read. You have to look. Look at those zigzags, those lozenges and spirals. Especially the spirals. Maggie said someone among those very first farmers was working out the escape route from the exigencies of living to the more accommodating realm of the stars. You can just imagine them reading those signs in the light of torches, during their ceremonies. And the spot they chose for their decorated stones. On the bold headland facing the restless immemorial power of the sea.'

The rough parking area of sand and stones was deserted at this hour of the morning except for a solitary ice-cream stall, boarded up. Our goal, the decorated passage grave, was encased in a turf-covered mound like a watch tower on top of the promontory that thrust out into the sea. The tide on the small beach below us was gentle enough, but the sea westwards was filled with a numinous power in the early morning light.

Pritch led the way up the narrow path alongside the headland, leaning heavily on his walking stick to relieve the arthritic pain in his right knee. In his haversack he carried his electric torch, his candles, a notebook and the key to the padlocked grill that guarded the entrance. He was followed, at a distance that could have been respectful or resentful, by the portly figure of Rod Roberts. I came last restraining myself from any untoward display of fitness. We could have been medieval pilgrims visiting a shrine or three schoolboys lining up to receive their certificates and prizes from the late Augustus Jones MA on his dais. I took time to pause and look back to admire my black BMW gleaming in solitary splendour in the crude deserted car park. It was a comforting sight.

When I caught up with the other two I found them gazing at a mobile phone lying crushed in a rain puddle between the modern retaining walls leading to the iron gate. Alongside the broken mobile lay the dispiriting shape of a discarded condom.

'Mind where you put your ancient feet,' Rod said in his jovial mode. 'You might catch something.'

The iron grill was not locked. The padlock was missing. Pritch muttered a curse on the irresponsible habits of tourists. The interior was pitch dark. Pritch was concerned with placing the candles where we could see the decorated stones to best effect. He gave Rod the electric torch to shine against the dome that covered the site.

'Good God,' Rod said. 'Prehistoric concrete.'

He began to sniff.

'Funny smell in here.'

Pritch was dissatisfied with the candlelight.

'You have to imagine flames from the torches. The spirals are the most difficult to make out. Shine a light over here, will you, Good God… is he dead?'

Underneath the special stone a male body dressed in a dirty overcoat lay in a foetal position. Rod went into action, happy to take charge.

'Not dead,' he pronounced. 'Drunk or drugged. Possibly both.'

It was alarming, unpleasant, but at least the man was not dead. If he had been, how on earth would we have managed? Rod poked around and shone the torch in his face; a young man, unshaven and unwashed and the distinctive smell could have been narcotic. He sat up slowly, yawning, peering about, bewildered in the candlelight.

'Jeesus,' he said. 'Somebody's birthday or what?'

A southern Irish accent I have always found charming. It came in strong contrast to the creature's smelly and scruffy appearance. Pritch was amused. He shone the torch on his own face and gave one of his more menacing grins.

'Mine,' he said.

The Irishman exaggerated his fear. It seemed to me he was acting more than reacting.

'Oh God,' he said. 'Dracula's Tomb. Where the hell are we?'

It was his business to explain himself. We waited in judgement and said nothing.

'In this wicked world, is there anything worse than liberated women? I was on my way to Holyhead with my guitar and, and they stopped their van to offer me a lift. The next thing I knew they were on about magic circles and moonlight and magic mushrooms and what have you and we landed here and the wicked bitches have nicked my guitar. Lovely guitar it was... oh Jeesus I'm bursting for a piss...'

'Outside then!'

Rod seemed to be in charge. We sat there in the candlelight until the dark figure reappeared in the entrance passage, blocking out the light at the end of the tunnel. Standing there he was a formidable, threatening figure so much stronger than the sleeping creature under the spiral stone.

'Is that your beautiful motor car down there?'

In the candlelight he could see my involuntary nod.

'Now isn't it a beautiful model? If I had a camera I would take a picture and maybe sell it to the papers!'

Rod cleared his throat. He was still determinedly in charge.

'You're on the run,' he said.

'Now why should you say that?'

The Irishman sounded quite hurt.

'I'm a magistrate,' Rod said. 'We're informed about these things.'

'Are you now?'

'A man with an Irish accent escaped from Presswood Open Prison three days ago. Or was it four.'

'Dear, dear.'

The Irishman gave a deep sigh and then a smile.

'The public are advised,' he said, 'to contact the police and not to approach him. Especially three old men.'

In a matter of seconds he produced a flick knife and held it to my throat.

'Now if you'd just hand me the keys of the car, I'd be off in the twinkling of an eye and trouble you no more. I'll be one careful driver.'

He had more to say as I fumbled for my keys but before he could say it Pritch had slammed the thick end of his walking stick into the side of his head, Rod had stamped on his hand and half the candles went out. The man lay moaning on the ground.

'Now what did you go and do that for,' he whimpered.

Pritch shone the torch in his face and he groaned even more.

'You're a monster,' he said. 'I'm maimed for life.'

I was still trembling from shock. For once I would not be the one to make the arrangements.

'What are we going to do with him?'

Rod was examining the flick knife in the poor light as if it were some new type of scalpel. He slipped it in his jacket pocket.

'Let him go,' he said. 'We're not policemen. I don't think he'll get very far.'

Together we pushed him down the entrance passage and watched him stumble down the steep slope, nursing his hand. In the parking ground he stopped to give my BMW a vicious kick before running on to the main road.

'Team work!'

I said it triumphantly although I knew I had done very little. They were the heroes of the hour. It did strike me however that in all the years we had known each other, this could be the very first time we had acted in concert. That had to be a cause for celebration. Out in the open we sat on the turf mound and I wanted to make a pleasantry about being too old for Old Boys Matches, that sort of thing. But Rod looked tired and defeated, fed up, now the excitement was over; and Pritch was cross that whatever he wanted to demonstrate had been spoilt by an unseemly intrusion.

'Disgusting,' Pritch said. 'The fact is you've seen very little standing stones and decorated stones. And there are twenty cromlechi on the island.'

'Place is covered with stone sermons.'

Rod was turning sarcastic.

'And how many chapels and how many churches? The fact is you've left it late in the day Mr Pritchard. You should have started your exploration of superstition at least fifty years ago.'

My heart sank. They were launching into a fierce argument about religion. In my business career that was one subject to avoid. I felt a strong desire to drop into the office at Philips Partners. Nothing more soothing than the sight of things nicely ticking over. Unfortunately I would need to take a grumpy Rod back to Llandeilo before I could get there. Old age was not enough to share in common. Our lives had run in parallel, but for the life of me I couldn't remember whether parallel lines met in infinity or not.

A Little History

HISTORY comes to an end when you stop breathing, my mother said and knowing her I think I know what she meant. It was not some version of solipsism: the world ceases to exist when I do. History comes to an end when you can't do anything about it. That's what she always believed and that's why she dragged me off to Greenham Common to shiver for days and even weeks on end outside that ghastly fence.

'Look at it girl!' she said.

'If you must rage against something, rage against these missiles! There will be no light for you and yours, girl, unless we do something about it.'

The drill was always to be aware of what was going on and always be ready to do something about it. And that's why I suspect she arranged for me to be conceived on that moonlit night in early November 1952.

***

It was quite a contrast really for those who bothered to notice. Their backgrounds are so different, it was noted in the staff room, when the news of their relationship leaked out. What they had in common, it was surmised, had to be a thoughtfulness and a shy withdrawal from boisterous contact, so different from the general run of sixth formers. Zofia didn't cling to ridiculous gossiping about boys, and Ifan was absent minded and had no taste for horseplay. Zofia Worowski was a year older than Ifan Roberts and in the opinion of some teachers too old to be still at school. Ifan, it was generally agreed, had always been too old for his years and heavily under the influence of his mother and even more of her father, a retired minister who made his home at the farm. A pretty boy had developed into a handsome youth, they said, but he spoiled this effect by always looking worried at an age when a healthy lad, the heir to a useful farm like Maen Bedo, should not have a care in the world. Zofia was more entitled to look worried. She was blonde and tall (at least an inch taller than Ifan), not beautiful in any conventional sense, but she moved well, conscious because of her height, of the need to be poised and graceful. But, apart from her brains, it seems she had little to fall back on. It was 1952 but in some respects she was still a refugee.

Mr Worowski, it was mooted abroad, had been in Polish Intelligence. That could have meant he had been a spy, but for whom and on whom Ifan had been too polite to inquire. When Zofia was four or five the family fled from Poland. Her father had been imprisoned in Moscow for two years and, he claimed, tortured. When he was released they moved to somewhere awful in Siberia and that's where her little

brother, Karol, died. She remembered train journeys that
went on forever and ever and she could still hear the clank
of the engine and wheels and the shaking and shuddering,
sometimes in her sleep. Then came the agreement between
the Soviets and the Polish government-in-exile in London.
This time the family moved to Persia, so that Mr Worowski
could join the Polish element in the British Army. Zofia went
to school in Palestine. Just as the Jewish-Arab war broke out
they moved from Gaza to Egypt; and then to London and to
Birmingham where things did not work out. Now they were
more or less settled in the Polish colony-camp outside
Pendraw and Zofia was in her last year in the grammar
school. Mr Worowski was still set on getting to America, but
he had developed heart trouble and it seemed unlikely he
would ever get there.

To Ifan, Zofia Worowski was a revelation. After an
innocuous school debate on literature and music, they went
on arguing on the way to the bicycle shed, if arguing is the
appropriate word. Zofia held forth and Ifan listened. A girl,
whom he had hardly ever heard speak before, was telling him
that music was the highest art not merely because it could
touch the sunshine but because it was abstract and had the
unique power to cross linguistic cultural ethnic boundaries.
It all seemed more significant because of her accent, which
he assumed to be central European. It was a culture in itself.
It may well be, she said, that individual words had more
magic than single notes, but what was the use of that when
a word was trapped, caged, in a single language? Cycling

home, Ifan was disturbed and even troubled by Zofia's pronouncements. They touched a nerve. He was besotted with Cymric strict metres and, taught initially by his grandfather, he had become quite skilled in the art; but as things stood, this superior intelligence that had invaded his life would never understand let alone appreciate his efforts.

A dialogue came about that both urgently needed. It seemed so amusing when Zofia pointed out they were both pontificating about meanings in English which was a second language to both of them and, in her case, a third. Ifan said that should make their arguments more precise. Wasn't it true that traditional scholars argued in Latin, wherever they came from? This seemed something of a joke too, and as their friendship developed the world around them grew brighter and more amusing. In a provincial society caught between hankering after an old tried and tested way of life and a growing appetite for prosperity and progress, they were able to make their own discoveries of the miracle of being young and alive. That summer of 1952 they explored the seashore together, visited ruins and churches, cycling through the green countryside and reaching a level of communication they sensed was higher than any other they had experienced. They seemed to question everything with an assumed objectivity that would have done credit to a pair of ageing dons.

People noticed of course and snide remarks were made in and out of school. It was a time and place when male and female were assumed to associate for one purpose only. Any remarks overheard, nods, winks and whispers, only served to confirm to Zofia and Ifan that they had moved to a higher level of existence. At the same time they were self-critical and modest in a manner they felt appropriate to a gifted elite.

Ifan was anxious for Zofia to meet his grandfather. There was one fount of wisdom and understanding to be compared with another. Tensions that had arisen in his mind between views that sometimes seemed to conflict could only be solved by a face-to-face encounter between the two sages. At Maen Bedo, a family farm that had a view of the bay and was beginning to expand a caravan site on rough ground with access to the beach, the Reverend Hughes, Taid, took refuge in a study bedroom that was lined with books. On most mornings Ifan brought him his early morning cup of tea. Mrs Roberts took quiet pleasure in the bond that existed between her father and her son. There was a similar quality in the pride she took in both. Her husband Gwilym wished the boy took a greater interest in the farm and the caravan site in the disused quarry by the shore and the daily pressures of profit and loss. If he had brains, as everybody said, it was important they should be put to good use. 'High thinking and plain living' exemplified by his father-in-law were all very well, but philosophy and literature had never been known to pay the rent. He respected the image of the cultured farmer, that was a tradition in Lleyn and Eifionydd, but it only worked in the real world if the prototype in question was as good at judging an animal and ploughing a furrow as he was at knocking out an englyn.

It took Ifan a little while to summon up the courage to ask his mother whether he could invite Zofia Worowski to tea at Maen Bedo. He declared that the brightest girl in the upper sixth was anxious to meet his illustrious grandfather, and he covered up this piece of wishful thinking by claiming 'she was very keen to understand local history', which sounded more plausible.

'And she's learning Welsh,' Ifan said.

'So she should,' was Mrs Roberts' instant reply. Then as was her custom she took her time to consider an unusual request.

'Well, I don't know. I shall have to ask your father.'

This was the standard evasion he had heard all his life. In social matters it was always his mother who made up his father's mind for him. She had been a schoolteacher before marrying a farmer and as a minister's daughter she was accustomed to taking a prominent position in the affairs of the chapel. She would also consult her father on what she took to be a matter of some delicacy.

'Who's this young lady, Ifan, that you've made friends with?'

The Reverend Hughes addressed his grandson in the cheerful broad-minded manner he used when asking questions that could sound inquisitive or intrusive. He was blessed with rosy cheeks and curly white hair and a honeyed voice that could command a singing tone when the occasion demanded it.

'Zofia Worowski, Taid. A really clever person. Physics, Chemistry and Maths but she could do anything really. In schoolwork I mean. Very interested in philosophy and she says she's eager to learn Welsh. I wanted you to meet her. That's why I want to ask her to tea.'

'Nothing of a sentimental nature then?'

'Not at all. We just have all these interests in common. That makes us good friends. In a way you could say it's just an accident that she happens to be a girl.'

His grandfather suppressed a smile. There were humorous points he would have enjoyed making about the nature of accidents and the accidents of nature, but the boy was anxious and this was not the time to make them. Ifan was enthusiastic and he had talents that needed to be nurtured. He was a sensitive plant. There was also the problem that being Polish, the girl would certainly be Catholic and although the Reverend Hughes was widely read and broad-minded, he was very wary of lingering prejudice in the chapel and indeed throughout the denomination. In those early fifties, in Welsh-speaking Wales, Catholicism was still anathema to nonconformist and socialist alike.

It took some time for all the objections to be overcome. The exams were over and so was the hay harvest and similar obstacles. Subject to results that the staff room considered a foregone conclusion, Zofia was expected to do medicine in Liverpool and Ifan to do languages in Bangor. The adult world was within reach and it seemed the perfect time for her visit. He was quite put out when Zofia declined the invitation. They were sitting on the green mound beneath Cricieth Castle when she said it wouldn't be a good idea.

'It would spoil things.'

They should have been contemplating the wondrous beauty of the bay and the majesty of the hills on such a fine summer afternoon. Harlech Castle on its rock was visible through a pale haze. Ifan had lines written about it all he wanted to repeat to her, but the invitation had to be made first.

'I'm foreign really, as well as strange. From what you've told me your parents are very...'

'Very what?'

'Conventional. Chapel and all that.'

'You've never met my grandfather. You can't imagine anyone so – open minded.'

'Later on perhaps, Ifan. When we've both been away, more independent.'

Ifan was upset. This became their first disagreement. He argued there was no theory or principle involved. It was just a simple invitation to tea. Zofia shook her head in sorrowful puzzlement. He was so upset she had to make a further effort to explain.

'You are the apple of their eye. They won't see me fit for your company. Where I come from is too far away and that makes me too unknown for them. You are their ideal. They would see me as spoiling your image.'

A precious summer afternoon was fading away into futile argument and silences and sulks. Before they cycled their separate ways, Zofia realised the relationship she valued hung by the slender thread of an invitation to tea. She had to accept.

It was the end of a week of warm, close weather and Zofia wore a bright floral frock for the occasion. The dominant red in her frock contrasted with the muted greys and browns of the farmhouse interior. Farmer Gwilym seemed happy to welcome a splash of colour. Zofia had shown an intelligent interest in the age of the farm buildings and their history. Mrs Roberts was far less pleased with the girl's appearance alongside her Ifan. She was an inch taller which seemed inappropriate and this made her look older and more sophisticated than her angelic son. Surely there were better-looking girls around with authentic Cymric connections? Her son deserved better. Whether Zofia understood or not she muttered to her husband as he came into the kitchen.

'She looks old enough to be his mother.'

The parlour table was laden with a farmhouse tea, everything proudly home-made from the bread and the butter to the delicate ham sandwiches, sponge cakes and scones. In time-honoured custom, Ifan was dispatched to the bottom of the ancient staircase to inform his Taid that Tea was ready. The Reverend Hughes made a benevolent entrance, bowing to the guest and proceeding to his chair at the head of the table with the same dignity that he ascended a pulpit. The initial politenesses were shy and uncertain. Ifan had never heard his Taid hold forth in English before. He became seismically sensitive to any reaction that could pass across Zofia's face. Did the old man sound stilted and even pompous? Her expression remained politely attentive. Inevitably the conversation turned to the aftermath of war.

The Reverend Hughes felt obliged to place events in historical perspective and in doing so made clear his own pacifist convictions. He attributed the ruthless increase in error and destruction to the licensing of bombing from the air.

'There was a disarmament conference you know in the nineteen twenties that wanted to outlaw bombing from the air. Great Britain objected. It needed to bomb natives on the north-west frontier. In the name of law and order. Now the Chinese invented gunpowder many many centuries ago. But they considered it too barbaric, too uncivilised for warfare, so they reserved it for fireworks. We could have done the same in the West for bombing from the air. But we didn't. And within two decades what do we get? The atomic bomb.'

The theorem concluded, he dissected a scone, placing a segment firmly in his mouth and chewing delicately. He glanced at the young persons in turn and smiled as if inviting comment. They remained thoughtful and silent. Gwilym felt obliged to speak.

'I don't know,' he said. 'These things go too deep for me. It takes me all my time to keep this farm going. What does your father think, Miss... Zofia?'

'My father? My father says if the Nazis got here we would be the first to be hanged from the nearest lamp post. Or tree should I say?'

She smiled to show she was prepared to discuss her father's conviction lightly. The effect was quite the opposite. The Reverend Hughes looked rebuffed and even offended.

Ifan was so disturbed he could barely sit still in his chair. It was an inescapable fact like a thunder clap; a world-wide war, the obliteration of cities, the death of millions, had been necessary to preserve the peace and tranquillity of Maen Bedo and its way of life. In one moment all he had heard from his grandfather was rendered obsolete. If that were the case would the compass of his life be left with anything he could call his magnetic pole? Everything was relative and beyond human control and there was nowhere he could stand and say he could do no other. He felt ignorant and lost.

'And what does your mother think?' Mrs Roberts said.

She had no taste for abstract discussion. That was what men engaged in when their stomachs were full and they had nothing better to do. She would draw her own conclusion by ascertaining a few basic actualities.

'I wouldn't know,' Zofia said. 'My parents are divorced.'

The interval of silence was long enough to express shock and even disapproval.

'Really.'

This was all Mrs Roberts could think of saying to dispel the silence.

'She works for a music publisher in London,' Zofia said. 'Before the war she had a musical career as an oboeist. In Warsaw. Of course I don't remember any of that.'

Everyone around the table was attempting an agreeable smile as if no-one would hold Zofia responsible for the tribulations of history.

'And you stayed with your father.'

Mrs Roberts spoke in a neutral tone, not ready to praise or condemn.

'Somebody had to look after him.'

'Fair play to you, girl!' Gwilym said, happy to demonstrate his approval.

Ifan looked at his father with greater affection than usual. His rough translation of a friendly blessing was a positive contribution.

Zofia was pressed to eat and expressed deep admiration for her piece of sponge cake.

'So light,' she said.

'Light as a feather,' added Ifan and they both laughed as though they had jointly composed a witty compliment. The Reverend Hughes recovered quickly in the warmer atmosphere. He was ready to expound further.

'It's not a pleasant thought,' he said. 'But it seems possible we are on the threshold of the first atheistic age in the history of mankind. Man has always believed in one god or another. He has to worship something. If we cease to believe, where do we anchor our moral code? What kind of religion justifies Hiroshima? A false religion, we say. A religion of power; the power of destruction and the power of money. Not a cheerful prospect. Now you young people must become the conscience of mankind. We call this the year of our Lord, nineteen fifty two but the danger is it is not His anymore.'

Ifan could see that Zofia was listening to his grandfather intently. The visit could be turning into the success he had hoped for.

'We have to struggle, don't we,' Zofia was saying. 'There is a struggle ahead to survive!'

It seemed to Ifan that the two wisest people he knew were in sufficient agreement. His mental compass, which had wobbled so violently, was beginning to stabilise. There would be a way ahead.

It emerged within a few weeks that Zofia and Ifan had both won prestigious scholarships. Mrs Roberts' pride in her son knew no bounds. She could not at all see why the boy hadn't gone to Oxford or Cambridge, they sounded so much nicer. She comforted herself that the young people were just good friends, associated by brilliance, without any dangerous romantic intentions. She was pleased when Ifan insisted that Bangor would provide the best grounding for the studies he needed to reinforce his literary ambitions. She began to nurse a secret hope that one day she would see her son both chaired and crowned at the National Eisteddfod.

Going their separate ways at the end of September Ifan and Zofia were cheerful enough. They were looking forward to fresh experiences that would deepen their understanding of the world. They would keep in touch as closely as they could and they would pass on any fresh insights as enthusiastically as ever. Bangor and Liverpool were outside cycling range, they joked, but part of their scholarships could be set aside for train fares. It didn't take many weeks for disappointment to set in. In the case of Ifan brought up on a farm and well used to amusing himself, reserved and circumspect by nature, he did not share the undergraduate

relish for companionship and company. He lingered watch-
fully on the margins and was not impressed with what he
saw. The literary societies appeared to be obsessed with
polishing traditions and criticising follies of the past about
which little could be done in any case, and bunkering down,
he felt, against the winds of change. In Liverpool, for her
own reasons just as retiring as Ifan, Zofia was surprised by
the lack of interest in a world that she knew was fraught with
dangers; the few women were intent on their careers and the
men absorbed with sports and bent on proving how manly
they could be. A post-war dust still lay heavily over the place
and the people.

Solitude compelled them to realise how much they
depended on each other. They were so busy that summer
being bright and objective they had never displayed any
affection for each other. Let alone use the language of love.
A new restraint entered their discourse. They had begun to
feel more than they could put into words and this in itself
sharpened the pains of solitude. What they could not express
to each other they could barely formulate to themselves.
There were telephone conversations that came to a troubled
halt. An eagerly awaited meeting in a shelter in the prom-
enade in Llandudno ended in a misery of misunderstanding.
The helplessness of the wider world had become a virus
infesting them too. Neither could find a way to declare
openly being unable to live without the other.

★★★

Zofia describes: I was early. It was an absolutely still day. I remember the sun setting, leaving an afterglow behind the black promontories and the bay was like a great gold undulating parchment and the water at my feet so clear, the ebb gently sucking at the small stones, and for the first time I felt a deep attachment to the place. We couldn't go on living unwittingly. This place, this relationship has become the centre of my being. The line of my life has been drawn across continents to be planted here. Here and now is everything. That's settled and I'm settled.

The caravans we had been inclined to despise and make fun of, were behind me. Closed and after season. But not closed to us if I followed out my intention. It wasn't all that cold. I was shivering from nervousness and fear. I knew by this that I loved Ifan, but I couldn't be certain he loved me in the same way. He was deeply attached of course, dependent even, but more perhaps to a muse than to a person? He was at times as abstract as a musical phrase, his head in the clouds, and of course that made him all the more precious to me. He not only looked like a poet, he was a poet. But unworldly. He was a farmer's son and must have been acquainted early with the facts of life and reproduction but I doubted whether he had any knowledge of human female anatomy and physiology: his parents were far too old-fashioned ever to have enlightened him.

I was watching the stencilled edge of the mountains merging gently into a dusky blue sky and the first star appearing when Ifan came up behind me. We had our rough bench sheltered by the edge of the old quarry. There was a bell ringing far away by the harbour. Ifan was too distressed to apologise for being late.

'The Americans have set off a hydrogen bomb! An island in the Pacific a mile long burnt for six hours and then evaporated. That's our world for you. Elect a President and let him blow up the world. It's not the superhuman dictator that will tear the world to bits. It's the fears and angers of little mister nobody, the democratic voter...'

'And rocks melt in the sun...'

I thought the line would calm him down. He was so full of his anxieties he barely heard.

'What are we except a species of mass murderers? The world would be better off without us. All we are good for is creating weapons of mass destruction. At least if we killed ourselves we wouldn't wipe anything else out. Suicide makes sense. When there's absolutely nothing else we can do about it.'

He sounded desperate enough to do anything. He looked cornered. Trapped. Unaware of what he was staring at.

I had to take the gamble. I couldn't let him escape me. I needed him too much. Being together was so much more important than any career.

'Yes, there is,' I said. 'Something we can do.'

I didn't use the world 'love'. For the first time I took him in my arms and we clutched at each other, desperate with inexperience. Clinging to each other still, we stumbled to a caravan. Damp as it was our excitement and ardour warmed it. I was as patient as Ifan was eager. As I feared he failed to penetrate me the first time. But he was so humble and enthusiastic I could only love him more.

***

And that is how I was conceived. That mundane and mysterious moment when the process of our existence begins. So commonplace, so bathetic, of no significance to anyone except one's solitary self. That's true of all life I suppose. It might not have happened, but it did and we spend the rest of our lives wondering what to do about it, until the corpse is made ready to be laid in the earth. Not however in Zofia's case. My mother spent her entire life struggling, protesting and arranging protests. In our family, history is made of milestones in her long march. My dear father abandoned his literary ambitions to nurture Maen Bedo and develop the caravan park with the success that made his wife's life of protest possible. The skill in the strict metres remains only a hobby. There were language protests too, but the beastly bomb was always at the centre of her preoccupations: the Cuban crises (I came home from school crying the world was coming to an end at three o'clock); the Berlin crises, an incident here an accident there, Greenham Common and the Trident protests. Right up to her death she kept banging on.

'That nuclear Non-Proliferation Treaty. What the hell are they doing about it?'

History made me, but I'm no legend. All I can do is accept the joke and carry on protesting. Whether or not it means anything, without having any effect. I shall never know, unless I find out after I stop breathing. But at least it's my life. It was given to me. I have no other.

Acknowledgements

The Grudge, Rendezvous, Luigi, Vennenberg's Ghost and *Nomen*, have previously been published in *Planet*

The author is deeply grateful to M. Wynn Thomas for assembling this collection and for his help and encouragement over many years.

About the Author

One of Wales' most celebrated authors, Emyr Humphreys was born in 1919 in Prestatyn, Flintshire.

As a conscientious objector, he served as a war relief worker in the Second World War. After working as a teacher, BBC drama producer and lecturer, he became a full time writer in 1972.

During a distinguished writing career he has won the Somerset Maugham Award for *Hear and Forgive* (1952), the Hawthornden Prize for *A Toy Epic* (1958) and several major Welsh Arts Council awards. In all he has published twenty-one novels as well as short stories, plays, poetry and essays, and is regarded as a major figure in post-war writing.

Emyr Humphreys novels published by Seren include *A Toy Epic, Outside the House of Baal, Unconditional Surrender, The Gift of a Daughter* (Welsh Book of the Year 1998), *Old People are a Problem, Ghosts and Strangers* and *The Shop*.